ANOTHER LIFE

D Gourlay

CONTENTS

ACKNOWLEDGMENTS

To my darling husband,
Thank you for not divorcing me considering the amount of
nights I spent completely ignoring you while researching, writing
or editing this book.
Thank you for believing in me and pushing me to believe in
myself.
I love you.

To Charlie, Cerri, Georgia, Mandy, Kayley, Natalie and every one
of my Baby Mamas, especially Kerri, Jo and Sarah. I would
never ever have got to this point without all of your help and
advice.
Thank you for everything.
I love and appreciate every single one of you.

COPYRIGHT

CHAPTER ONE

Rachel

I can't believe how quickly the summer has gone.   One minute I was outside sunbathing while Amelia swam around in her little pool, shouting for me to get in with her; the next I'm searching the cupboards for the winter quilts at 3am as my toes feel like they have turned to ice.

I hear a bang and tip toe over to Amelia's room to check she is ok. Sound asleep. As I'm creeping back to my room I hear another bang. What on earth is that noise? The spare room is empty, Kevin must still be working, or staying out of town, or out with his friends, hell if I know.

Bang! Bang! BANG!

"RACHEL"

Oh fuck.

"Rachel, for Christ sake get your fat arse down here and open the fucking door!"

Well I guess that explains where Kevin was, out getting drunk. Brilliant, drunk Kevin, just what I needed. Maybe I should just leave him out there, all I'm going to get when he walks through that door is a torrent of abuse anyway.

BANG! BANG!

"RACHEL! I SWEAR TO FUCKING GOD OPEN THIS DOOR NOW!"

If he carries on he is going to wake Ami, I'm going to have to let him in and hope he passes out sooner rather than later. I rush down the stairs and can see his face pressed up against the glass on the door.

"There you are! For fuck sake open the door, or is that too difficult for you?"

Oh joy. As soon as the door opens, a strong smell comes wafting into the house. A disgusting mix of alcohol, stale cigarette smoke and sweat.

"What took you so fucking long?"

He's slurring his words, his eyes totally bloodshot, his usually sleek blonde hair is a complete mess. His shirt buttons are done up wrong and he hasn't even bothered doing his trousers up. His lips look swollen, like he's been engaged in a long session with some little slut. The man standing in front of me is a shadow of the man I met all those years ago.

"Jesus look at the state of you. Where have you been?"

He takes my face in his hand and brings my face closer to his. The smell of alcohol on his breath is so strong it almost makes my eyes water.

"None of your fucking business." He growls at me.

"I'm supposed to be your wife, of course it's my business!"

He just ignores me and staggers over to the sofa. He barely makes it before falling on to it. He swings his legs up, lays down and looks like he's going to pass out straight away. A silent wave of relief flows through me; that wasn't so bad. Usually he spends a good ten or twenty minutes screaming awful things at me when he gets back in this state. Which lately has been at least twice a week. I silently turn around when I hear him start laughing to himself. I turn to look at him and he is staring at me, laughing.

"You know, for a second I thought maybe you had another man in the house and that's what took you so long to open the damn door!" He roars with laughter and struggles to speak.

"But honestly, I'm not sure there's a single man out there who would find your fat arse a turn on!"

I storm off and can hear him giggling to himself like a drunk moron even from the top of the stairs. I walk into my room and close the door behind me, my own little safe haven. He hasn't stepped foot in this room for years now. I remember a time when that little episode would have reduced me to tears. I'd have come running up here a sobbing mess, but not anymore. That's not me now, it's all water off a ducks back. In the morning he probably won't even remember. He will make some shitty comment about his coffee not being warm enough or he doesn't want what I've made for breakfast; and then he will storm off to work and I'll see him when he decides to come home again.

Part of me worries about the effect this has on Amelia, but she's out of the house so much with school, clubs and friends; and Kevin is out so much working, or whatever the hell he gets up to in his spare time. So I don't think she really notices there is anything wrong. She's only nine, but she is so grown up for a nine year old. She is my shining ray of sunlight through the absolute shit storm her dad puts me through. And as much as I know I should leave for her sake, I know I can't. I can't risk losing her to him.

I'm so tired and have to be up soon, I need to shut my brain off for a little while and try to sleep. I set my alarm earlier than usual to check that idiot is off the sofa before Ami comes down in the morning.

CHAPTER TWO

My alarm sounds at 5.45am and I've managed maybe an hours sleep. I creep out of my room and can see Ami is still fast asleep. I can hear snoring coming from the guest room so I guess the drunkard made it up to bed at some point. My house smells of alcohol and cigarettes and- no. He'd better not have- I race down the stairs and yep, the bastard has thrown up all over the floor and just left it there. I needed coffee this morning, not to be cleaning up dried in vomit from my beautiful rug. God I hate him. I do not have the stomach for cleaning this up. The rug is going to have to go. I get a couple of bin bags and open them up, roll up my once gorgeous, soft rug and wrap it in the bags. I walk it outside and throw it straight in the bin.

I set about making a pot of coffee while making sure Ami has her bags packed. She is off to stay with my Mum and Dad for a few days, her school has an inset day today, and then all of next week is half term, so my parents are making the most of a free long weekend with her. She absolutely loves her grandparents and they dote on her. They spend as much time as they can with her and always spoil her, no matter how much I protest.

They take her out for burgers and ice cream, to the cinema, bowling. Whatever my little Ami wants, she knows that her Nanny and Gramps will sort it for her! I'm settling down with my coffee when I can hear excited footsteps running down the stairs. 6am on the dot, same as every day. That girl's body clock is insane!

"Mummy! Mummy! Mummy! Are Nanny and Gramps here yet?"

I laugh.

"Babe, its 6am, Grandpa is probably still snoring away in bed! Come here and give me a cuddle."

She skips over and wraps her arms around me. I hold her tightly in my arms and kiss her gently on the head. I take a deep breath in, smelling her sweet strawberry shampoo, and sigh. This little girl is my absolute world and she just melts me.

"Morning Mummy, did you sleep well?"

"I slept really well baby, what about you?"

"I slept good Mummy. Can I have pancakes for breakfast?"

"With Bacon?"

"Mmmm yes please! And syrup?" She licks her lips.

"No problem baby, you watch cartoons and I'll sort your breakfast."

"Yay! Love you!" she shouts at me, skipping towards the TV.

I can't remember ever having a maternal bone in my body as a child. I never played with baby dolls or longed for a baby brother or sister as my friends all did. I couldn't understand why anyone would want a baby! A little person, totally unable to do anything for itself. All they did was cry, and poo, and eat, and cry, and poo. Everyone I knew with a baby would constantly complain how they never got any sleep. It just sounded like my idea of hell. And the day I found out just *how* babies come into the world I vowed I would never put my poor bits through that! Even when I found out I was pregnant I didn't want a baby. I was so young. I was in college, I wanted to learn and get myself a good job, have a career. We were so careful, I was on the pill and me and Kevin always used condoms. Kevin was my first, and only for that matter. We met when I was sixteen, Kevin was twenty five.

He was so intense so early on. He would want to see me almost every day, would always buy me gifts and insist on paying for everything. He didn't like it if I went out with my own friends and didn't let him tag along. But he was gorgeous, had a good job, and seemed to genuinely care about me. So I held on, hoping he was just crazy for me and he would calm down in time. Turns out he was just crazy and things would only get worse...

Three months after we started seeing each other, on my seventeenth birthday he told me he loved me and asked me to move in with him. In front of all of my friends. I was far too young for that. I wasn't in love with him, hell I hadn't even ever referred to him as my boyfriend at that point. I told him that I was too young and it was too soon and could we just take things slowly. Things seemed to be going well. Then a few months later I went to the doctors as I'd had the flu for weeks and just didn't seem to be getting any better. I was so tired all the time, couldn't keep any food down. Well it turned out I was eight weeks pregnant. I was in complete shock, and asked my doctor immediately about abortions. I got home and texted Kevin. I couldn't bear to call him, to hear his voice. I knew that he would be happy about it, knew he would want to keep it and would try to convince me it would be a great idea. But I was so young. It just wasn't an option for me. He was always so caring and lovely with me that I hoped he would understand. He was so much older than me, he had lived his life and mine hadn't even really began yet.

"Please don't freak out, I've been to the doctor and I'm pregnant. I have no idea how. We were so careful. I'm far too young for this Kev. Can you come over so we can talk?"

I just needed to be firm with him. Explain that now was not the time, but who knew what the future might hold.

An hour later the doorbell went, mum got to the door first. Filling the door were flowers and balloons with "Congratulations!" and pictures of dummies and nappies on them. Kevin pushed them all aside to make room to get through the door and gave my very confused mum a hug.

"Congratulations Mary!"

My poor mum was baffled. I was watching this all from the top of the stairs. Frozen to the spot in anger. *He knows I don't want this baby, how dare he try to guilt me into keeping it.*

"Kevin dear, I've not been able to have babies for a while now! What is all this about?"

Something suddenly clicked on in my head and I started racing down the stairs, desperate to stop him telling my mum, she would never ever let me go through with an abortion, she could never know.

"Ha-ha Kevin, you're such a joker" I manage to butt in just as he's opening his mouth

"It's just Kevin's weird sense of humour mum, don't worry I don't get it either!"

Jeez that was a close-

"Don't be silly Rachel, your mum is going to be a Granny, she should be able to share the excitement with us."

I just stared at him open mouthed. How dare he do that to me? Looking back now, I should have ran as far away from him as possible. That was just the start of his bullshit.

I can hear stomping down the stairs that brings me sharply back into the present moment. He's up then.

"Morning princess, how did you sleep?"

As much of a complete knob he is to me, he is a decent Dad, when he is around that is. I'm just plating up everyone's breakfast when he walks into the kitchen.

"Where's my coffee?"

"In the coffee pot, I didn't pour you one in case it went cold."

He always complains that his coffee is too cold, or too warm, or too sweet, too milky, the list goes on. I can do no right with Kevin.

"You were a state last night, where had you been?"

I know I won't get the truth but it's worth an ask.

"Out."

No shit Sherlock, thanks for that.

Ami walks in smelling the bacon.

"Oh Mum, it smells yummy!"

That girl always manages to make me smile.

CHAPTER THREE

I'm stood outside the house waving as my parents drive away with Amelia. She loves it at their house and never wants to come home, but I absolutely hate it when she isn't here. It means it's just he and I in the house, alone. You could cut the atmosphere with a knife half the time or hear a pin drop in the silence the other half. He should be leaving for work soon though so I can go about my list of things to do without him getting in the way. It's surprisingly warm today compared to how cold it was last night, so I decide to mow the lawn before it gets too wet to be able to do.

He is sat on the sofa when I get in.

"Not going to work today?"

He completely ignores me.

"For God sake Kevin, we live in the same house, we are married. What is the point in either of us sticking around if you can't even be bothered to speak two words to me?"

He stands up angrily and skulks towards me, glaring.

"Yes we are married and you are my wife so show me a bit of fucking respect. No, clearly I am not going to work today or I would have left by now."

I can't stand this man. I don't think it is possible to hate anything more than I hate him. I pick up my bag and jacket and leave the house. The housework will have to wait for a day, I'm not spending the day at home alone with that piece of crap. I head off towards the beach. That's one good thing about living here; I'm only a five minute walk from everything, schools, shops, trains, and the most beautiful little secluded sandy beach that hardly anyone knows about. It's hidden behind some thick bushes in its own little cove that can't be seen from either side.

There are a few other people there when I arrive; a young couple walking a dog, a sulky teenager that looks like he is having a forbidden cigarette and a man sat with his head in his hands.

I know how he feels.

I walk towards the water, wanting to dip my toes in, but it's not that warm, there's a real breeze and it's blowing my hair all over the place. It's so quiet except for the waves, the breeze and the occasional yap of the couple's dog. Damn they look so happy, I don't think I've ever been that happy. Of course with Ami but that's a different kind of happy.

I gave birth to Ami the day before my eighteenth birthday. I spent my birthday in hospital, learning how to breast feed and bathe her. I'd been planning my eighteenth for years. I was so excited about it. Me and my friends were going to go into London and spend the night going from bar to bar and I was going to do eighteen different shots.

Mine and Kevin's parents visited the hospital with gifts for me and Ami, and it was then, in front of everyone that Kevin asked me to marry him and move in. I was too exhausted, mentally and physically, to be able to deal with all the questions and the kind of atmosphere that comes with a "no" so I said yes. We were married not long after, I remember crying for hours the night before telling my mum I didn't want to go through with it. I love my mum, but Kevin had worked his magic on her.

"Don't be silly darling, everyone gets cold feet. Kevin is amazing, he's wonderful to you and amazing with Amelia. Don't let nerves get in the way of the happiest day of your life."

None of what she said was untrue, back then he was lovely. But I couldn't help but feel like I'd had my life stolen away from me and resented him for that.

Tad

I don't know why I thought coming here would help. I haven't been here since I was a child. My Dad would bring my little brother Sebastian and I here for picnics and to kick a ball around. I always loved how quiet it was, all you could hear was the water lapping at the shore and the occasional bird, hardly anyone knew about our special little beach back then. It's been a month since my brother's funeral and I still can't believe that he has gone. It was so sudden. We had been on a night out with our friend Scott. The next day he was really suffering. We took the piss out of him, saying how he was getting old and couldn't handle his drink anymore. I left him at mine while Scott and I went out to get him hangover supplies, and by the time we got home he was passed out on the sofa barely breathing. He'd had a heart attack. My twenty nine year old, super fit, gym freak brother had a heart attack.

I sat next to his bed all night and woke up to him laughing at us saying he wasn't faking after all. My mum arrived at the hospital and the doctors then told us that a scan showed a defect with Seb's heart and he would need surgery. But he never made it. He had another massive heart attack later that day and they couldn't bring him back.

We had never been close to our Mum. Dad worked full time when we were growing up, and Mum was a housewife, but to be honest we hardly saw her. I was left to look after Seb most of the time, but it suited us just fine. Mum bounced back from his death pretty quickly. She even left his funeral early...

I am not coping so well. Seb was my best friend as well as my brother. We were polar opposites in terms of personalities, but we were so close. Luckily I work mostly from home so nobody knows just how hard it has hit me. I can't stand people staring, the looks of pity and the stupid smiles when they don't know what to say. I'd much rather hole up with some booze, take away and whatever shit is on the TV. But I needed to get out today. I was going to go to visit Seb's grave, but the closer I got, the more stressed out I felt, so I started walking the opposite way and ended up here.

It's not helping at all me being here so I lift my head out of my hands and start to stand up, and that's when I see her. A woman with long brown hair, sitting on the sand, hugging her knees. She looks exactly how I'm feeling. Her hair is blowing in the breeze and I can't help but stare at her. I wonder what her face looks like? I bet she is pretty.

As if she knows I'm staring at her she turns her head and looks at me. I can't move. She has the most beautiful face I've ever seen. Beautiful blue eyes, rosy cheeks and soft pink lips. She looks so sad, her eyes are red where she has clearly been crying. I have the overwhelming urge to go up to her to hug her, but I don't think she would be too happy about some weirdo staring at her and then hugging her. She turns away and stands up, her body matches her face; perfect. She starts walking away from the water, she glances over at me and throws a little smile my way. I smile back and put my hand up to wave. I've got this funny feeling in my stomach, it feels like it's doing summersaults, and my cock starts to stir too. Haven't felt like this in a while. Maybe I'll go and speak to her? Maybe I'll ask her out, a date might take my mind off things at least. But by the time I've got myself together I can't find her. I sit back down and resume my depressed stare out into space.

CHAPTER FOUR

Rachel

God what was that? I caught Mr. mysterious and moody staring at me when I was sat on the beach and I had to get away from there as quickly as possible. He was utterly beautiful. He had the most amazing eyes I'd ever seen, even from so far away I could make out how incredibly blue they were. Framed by long eyelashes that any girl would kill for. They were beautiful eyes, but sad. He had big bags under them that looked like he hadn't slept in a while. I don't know what it was about him, I only looked at him for a couple of seconds, but I felt my stomach jumping and a heat in between my legs I hadn't felt in years... I was so shocked I just got up and ran off. As I was leaving I saw him smile at me, his mouth was surrounded by stubble that I can imagine would really tickle if he were kissing me... Or licking me, down there...

Jesus Rachel calm down!

I'm hiding in an alley way trying to compose myself. What is wrong with me? Can't even be looked at by a good looking man without turning into a puddle apparently.

I've managed to calm myself down and have gone for a walk into town to do some shopping. My phone buzzes in my pocket and I pick it up to see Ami has sent me a snap, it's of her and my dad with flower halos! She is obviously having fun! I send her a text back-

Tell Grandpa that suits him! Hope you are having fun sweety x

As I go to come out of my messages I can see a message from Celine that has been read, but definitely not by me. That fucker has been reading my text messages again. How the hell did he get into my phone this time? I use the fingerprint unlock and have made my back up password so long and complicated even I struggle to remember it... Better change my passwords on everything again then. I read the message.

Hey gorgeous, why has it been so long? Seriously we need to catch up, I have sooo much gossip! When can you come over? Xx

Celine is my absolute best friend. We met at primary school and she has been like a sister to me. She is the only person that knows almost every detail of my life, including all the shit with Kevin that I hide from everyone else.

Sorry babe, I didn't see your message. Ami is at mums for a few days so I can do lunch tomorrow? Xx

I put my phone back in my bag and wander around the shops. I have £35 left of the 'allowance' that Kevin gives me and he gets paid tomorrow so I will get my monthly £300 then. That money is supposed to buy Ami clothes, pay for school bits and clubs, buy her lunches, and pay my phone bill, car insurance and petrol. He worked it all out and that was the number he came up with.

I have no money for myself, if I want anything I have to ask him for the money and give him a good reason for it. Of course occasionally when he comes home totally off his face with his wallet bulging with twenty pound notes I make sure a few of them go missing. He is always so drunk he has never noticed. I figure I'll treat myself to coffee and a cake before heading off shopping as I have a bit of money going spare. I head into Costa and order myself a large caramel latte and a slice of carrot cake.

It is rammed in here, there a few old ladies in for their tea and scones while they talk about various medical appointments they are off to, and the rest of the tables seem to be occupied by students who have only come in here to plug their laptops in and abuse the free Wi-Fi. There is a little table in the back corner free, so I take my tray and go and sit down. I grab my phone out and start flipping through Facebook, my mum has put about twenty photos up of my Dad and Ami making cakes together. A message flashes up on screen from Celine –

I can't do tomorrow babe, have a hot fucking session planned tonight at a nice hotel and don't plan on being able to walk tomorrow ;) I can do Sunday though? Xx

I laugh to myself, typical Celine! She has been with her boyfriend for almost a year now, they are hardly ever apart, and they can't keep their hands off one another. Even when we get the occasional girly time together they are constantly on the phone to one another.

Celine says it was love at first sight, they first saw each other on a packed train heading into London, by the time the train got in at Paddington they had exchanged numbers, by the time they had left the station they had arranged to go out for drinks that evening, and by the end of the night they had decided they were going to spend the rest of their lives together!

Ha-ha you minx! Say Hi to Danny for me. Sunday is fine babe, let me know where and when. Enjoy your night, not jealous at all! Xx

I put my phone on the table and pick up my coffee, and then out the corner of my eye I see Mr. mysterious and moody stood at the counter.

Tad

The smell of coffee fills my nose and makes my mouth water slightly as I'm waiting in line.

"Large double shot Americano to take out please"

Coffee will sort me out. Coffee is the answer to all the wrongs in the world. Well up until the point in the day where it becomes socially acceptable to drink alcohol instead... I pay up and wait for my drink and out the corner of my eye I see the beautiful woman from the beach. She is a lot closer now and I can see her better. Her skin is flawless, her hair is long, down past her shoulders and it's a beautiful chocolate brown colour. I turn back around quickly before she catches me staring at her for the second time today. I can see the barista putting my coffee into a mug. I'm sure I said to take away? I'm just about to ask her to tip it into a take away cup, when I notice that the only free table in the place is next to the girl from the beach.

Fuck it. I'll just have to drink it in here and I guess I will have to sit next to her as it's the only table free.

Divine intervention perhaps?

My coffee appears and I take it and walk over to her. She is sitting by the back wall on a bench that stretches for the length of the wall. There are two tables and she is at the furthest one. I walk through the middle of the tables to sit next to her at the back. She smells of apples and perfume, I take a deep breath and realise I'm being really creepy.

She has her head buried in her phone and she doesn't notice me sit down next to her. I pick up my coffee and take a long sip. I can see her drinking out the corner of my eye. I normally hate people, all people, I hate talking to them or being in a public place, but all I want to do is turn and say hello to this random stranger. This random beautiful, sexy stranger who I want in my bed.

I can feel my cock stirring in my trousers. Shit. What the fuck is going on, I don't know this woman's name, I haven't even said one word to her and already I'm imagining her naked riding on top of me. I go to put my coffee down and slip and manage to spill half my cup all over the table.

"Shit!"

Why does this always happen to me?

"Here, I've got loads of napkins."

I turn around to see her handing me a handful of napkins. I blush, why the fuck am I blushing? I haven't blushed since I was five.

"Thank you, it's been one of those days!"

She looks at me with a sympathetic smile, she has the most amazing blue grey eyes. They almost look silver in places. They are twinkling so much they remind me of tiny galaxies. She tucks a bit of hair behind her ear and there, glinting at me like a big 'fuck you' is a wedding ring.

"Don't worry about it, it's usually me spilling or dropping things!"

Even her voice is sexy.

A waitress comes over to mop up the last of the coffee. As she walks off, she not so subtly drops a napkin on the table. On the napkin is a note, *Call me* and her phone number. I hear giggles coming from next to me, she noticed that too then. I sigh and screw up the napkin.

"Not going to call her then?" She says with a wry smile.

"Well I didn't call her the first two times she dropped her number in my lap so I'm not sure why she thinks I'd call this time to be honest!"

"Third time lucky maybe?"

"Yeah not happening, I really thought she had got the message by now. I think I need to find a new coffee shop!"

"Maybe she is just hopelessly in love with you?"

She is giving me the cheekiest smile. She bites her bottom lip and it's the sexiest thing I've ever fucking seen.

"Or maybe she has just forgotten she already tried it on with me twice before? I'm sure she has just given her number to two other blokes in here."

Low and behold, she is over at another table, flirting with another customer and writing her number on another napkin.

She is laughing loudly now and it's infectious, I smile broadly.

"I wonder if management here know why they have to order so many extra napkins!" She giggles.

I'm actually laughing. I don't remember the last time I laughed. This girl has it all, looks, personality and the ability to turn my shit mood around.

17

Yes, and I bet her husband loves her for all of those things.

She turns to look at me,

"Well I'd better be going, it was lovely meeting you."

No. Don't go.

"It was lovely meeting you too. Thank you by the way."

"For what?"

"Well for the napkins, and for cheering me up, it's been a while since I laughed."

"Well I'm glad to have helped."

She smiles at me and brushes her hair behind her ear As she stands up I can see that she has the looks, personality, and body to go with it. Sexy curves, and a backside to die for. I can't help but imagine grabbing onto her arse while she is sitting on top of me, riding my cock... Fuck, I definitely have a hard on under the table.

"My name is Tad by the way." Well that came out of nowhere, I don't remember her asking for my name. "Just in case you were wondering..."

Oh my god, please just stop talking. She's smiling at me again.

"Tad?" She asks.

"Yeah, it's short for Thaddeus, but I only really get called that when I'm in trouble."

"Thaddeus. What a beautiful name. Doesn't that mean something along the lines of a gift from God?"

Body, looks, personality, and brains. Nobody ever knows what my name means, normally I get 'Oh what an odd name'.

"Yes, it does, nobody ever knows that!"

She looks down and smiles.

"Well, Tad, it was lovely meeting you. I'm Rachel. Maybe see you around some time."

And like a shot she is gone.

CHAPTER FIVE

Rachel

I run out of that coffee shop so fast that I almost take out a poor old man as I'm leaving. I mumble my apologies and hurry off round a corner. What was that? My heart was going so fast I thought it was going to beat out of my chest. Tad was gorgeous. Absolutely gorgeous. His eyes were the most brilliant blue I've ever seen. His voice traveled right through me and seemed to settle in the pit of my stomach, causing all sorts of butterflies. I really need to pull myself together. As sexy as he is, I'm married.

Yes I'm aware that I'm married to a total wanker, and that is half the problem. There is absolutely no way I could ever leave him, I'm terrified of what he would do.

But he fucks around, maybe I could too...

I stop my brain before it continues along this path. I am not a cheat, I have never and will never be a cheat. If we ever do end up divorced, I want to be the one who stayed true to her vows. I want to come out the better person. I don't want a single person to feel sorry for Kevin, or think he had any form of justification for the way that he treats me. So that's it. Strike Tad from my mind, find a new coffee shop and move on with my life.

Suddenly my phone starts going off in my bag, bringing me back to the real world. *Kevin.*

Oh fuck, this can't be good.

"Kevin."

"Rach I need you home, we're going out."

"Well thanks for the notice. What if I had plans?"

"Don't really give a damn if you had plans. There's a fundraiser tonight, black tie, fancy pants meal. I can't go alone. I RSVP'd for you too."

"How long have you known about this?! Why didn't you tell me sooner? I can't just pull an outfit suitable for a black tie event out of nowhere you know?"

This is so like Kevin, clicks his fingers and just expects me to run. And of course I do go running.

"It doesn't matter how long I've known, just get home. I've got you an outfit sorted already. We are leaving at 7, be ready."

Oh great. An evening with all of his snotty work friends playing happy families.

Tad

'm home and I can't stop thinking about Rachel. She is just perfect. Maybe she isn't married. Maybe she just wears a ring on that finger.

A wedding ring...

Ok so she is married. Or maybe she was married, maybe he died. I smack myself in the head, I'm now wishing some poor bloke dead because I think his missus is stunning. My phone goes off in my pocket. *Susan.*

"Hey Suzie, what's up?"

"Where are you?"

"Umm I'm at home. Why?"

"Why are you at home? You are supposed to be getting ready at the Four Seasons- Wait home as in not even in London yet? THADDEUS!"

Oh shit. The fundraiser. That is tonight.

"Oh shit, Suze, don't hate me, I forgot. I've had a really shitty couple of days"-

"Stop. I don't want your excuses. Your suit is here, your speech is here. You need to get here in the next hour to get ready, understood?"

I check my watch, its already 5pm. 5pm driving into London, traffic nightmare.

"Suze I'm leaving now OK. I'm running. Please don't leave me!"

"I swear there had better be a bloody big Christmas bonus coming my way this year. You would never be able to replace me you know, nobody would put up with you."

"I know Suze, best PA mug coming to you for Christmas..." I hear a snort down the phone. "Filled with fifties?" I add quickly and she laughs. I'm off the hook.

"That's more like it. Now seriously, get your backside here now!"

"See you in an hour Suze."

Shit, shit, shit. How could I forget? It's the annual fundraiser for the Police Dependents Trust tonight. It's my fundraiser, I organized it! Well I leave all that sort of stuff to Suzie but it is probably quite important that I am there, and as one of the charities biggest patrons I have to make a speech. Usually this would be the kind of thing me and Seb would go to together. I quickly grab my phone charger, wallet and keys and leave before my mind gets a chance to think about him too much.

CHAPTER SIX

Rachel

I don't even want to think about where he got this dress from. Or who helped him choose it. I mean, it's a gorgeous dress. Stunning. It's strapless, red, covered in sequins and has a slit from the bottom right up to my thigh. It's just beautiful. I wonder if he's borrowed this from someone he has been shagging. Or if he took one of his whores out to help him choose it...

I'm almost done putting my make up on, I've put my hair up in a loose chignon and have gone for smoky eyes and red lips. I stare at myself in the mirror and wonder what Tad would think of how I looked. Jeez how ridiculous. Literally only spoken to the guy for two minutes and now I'm sat fantasising about him. Kevin knocks on my door.

"Rachel, the cab will be here in five. Are you ready?"

I sigh. He will be nice to me on the way there to put me in a good mood, to make me think we are going to have a lovely evening as man and wife. He will probably hold my hand as we walk into the building, he will no doubt plaster a smile on and act the doting husband whilst in front of the any paparazzi and everyone there. And then when we get home he will go back to being a complete arsehat.

"Yeah, I'm just coming."

I open the door to see Kevin stood in a tux. His blonde hair is styled perfectly to the side, and he is clean shaven showing off his chiseled chin. He looks great. He always looks great in a tux. He is holding a little blue box in his hand.

"You look nice. What's that?"

He passes me the box.

"This is for you. Thought it would go nicely with the dress."

I open the box to find a beautiful necklace. It looks like white gold, with a big ruby in the middle. There are clusters of diamonds surrounding the ruby. It's stunning.

"Kevin..?"

I'm speechless. He is normally nice to me before we have to go somewhere but I can't remember the last time he got me a gift? Especially one this nice. Or expensive.

"I'm sorry I've been such a wanker recently. More so than usual. A job opening came up a few weeks back. Cut a long story short, you are now looking at the new Police and Crime Commissioner for Sussex Police."

"Oh wow Kev, that's amazing. Well done!"

He has wanted this job forever. It's a shit load of responsibility, and a shit load of money.

"£190k plus a year Rach!"

I'm speechless. I have no idea how he has landed this job. I'm sure there are people there more qualified, more experienced than him. It wouldn't surprise me if he has played dirty somewhere along the lines. But if he is happy, then maybe he will be happier at home? Maybe he will treat me a bit better? Maybe he is apologising for real?

Maybe you will open the front door to find a unicorn is flying you to London...

Time will tell I suppose.

The sound of the doorbell interrupts my thoughts. The cab must be here.

"I'll just grab my bag, meet you in the cab?"

He smiles at me and walks off down the stairs. Hang on, he smiled at me? He really is in a good mood.

CHAPTER SEVEN

Tad

Oh shit, she is mad.

"Thaddeus Turner, you are so late. And look at you, you haven't even shaved."

"Oh Suze, don't look at me like that. I know. I'm sorry! But you know what rush hour traffic is like around here."

"Just get in there, see Sam, he will do your hair and try to neaten up that birds nest on your face. Then you get changed at superman speed and meet me downstairs in twenty minutes. You got that? Twenty minutes. Not a minute more!"

"I'm going, I'm going!"

Susan Jones is not someone you want to get on the wrong side of!

I walk into my room and find Sam waiting for me with his chair and mirror all set up.

"Taddy Taddy! Where have you been my love?!"

"I'm sorry Sam, been a rough few days!"

"I don't think I've seen you since poor Sebby passed. How are you doing? Silly question darling I know. I'm just going to shut up now. Please take a seat my love. What is this on your face? I don't have time to get rid of this completely, but you are in luck, a little bit of face fuzz seems to be all the rage right now, plus you pull it off so well, you look all rugged, like a mountain man."

Sam is my stylist whenever I am in London. He and Susan go way back and she insisted that I needed someone to help me choose clothes and get ready for events. I did try to argue that I've been brushing my own hair and cleaning my own teeth since I was about four, but once Susan wants something, Susan normally just goes ahead and does it. I sometimes wonder who the boss actually is.

With one minute to spare I walk out of the lift into the foyer. Suze jumps out at me on the other side of the doors.

"Jesus woman you scared the crap out of me!"

"Stop talking. You need to sneak out of the rear exit and walk back around so you can come up the steps to have photos taken by the press."

"Oh Suze, you know I hate all that bullshit. Can't I just go in and wait inside for everyone?"

She doesn't say anything. She doesn't have to. She just looks at me over the rim of her little red half-moon specs and points in the direction of the exit.

I managed to find my way out and I'm walking round the side of the building. There are a couple of cars lining up in front of the hotel waiting for their passengers to come out. Brilliant, I will just sneak in behind a couple of people and the press won't even notice me. The door to a black Mercedes opens and I'm just about to try to sneak behind them when I see her.

Dressed in a beautiful red dress that hugs all of her curves, it's her. Rachel. What are the chances? Like a million to one, surely. And there, getting out of the cab behind her is some greasy blonde bastard. He puts his hand on the small of her back and leads her towards the entrance to the Four Seasons. She wraps her arm around his back.

I guess her husband is alive and kicking after all.

Damn.

Rachel

We walk into the Ballroom at the four seasons. There is a man holding a tray with flutes of champagne at the entrance, Kevin grabs one for each of us. He clinks his glass with mine and gives me a cheeky wink. Who is this man?

An older man walks up to us and I recognise him from a few other events I've been dragged to.

"Kevin! Congratulations Mr. Police and Crime Commissioner!"

"Thanks David, would never have got the job without your help though!"

"Ah you were the right man for the job Kevin, I just helped them see that."

He turns to me, takes my hand and kisses it.

"And might I say how beautiful you look tonight Mrs. Police and Crime Commissioner."

"Thank you David, it's lovely to see you again."

"You two will be sitting at my table at the front. The bar is over there, and don't forget to have a go on the silent auction! Kevin, do you mind if I borrow you for a moment? There's a few people I would like to introduce you to?"

"No problem, Rach I will meet you at the table ok?"

"Yeah ok, I will go and spend all of your new wages at the silent auction!"

David laughs at me and slaps Kevin on the back as they walk off.

"You've got a little firecracker there haven't you Kev!"

I wander over to the table where the items are being auctioned off. There are a few hampers with wine and various foods. There are vouchers for hair salons and beauty treatments, a weekend break away at the Four Seasons, and a long weekend to Paris. I put a couple of small bids down on a few things, just to look like I'm participating, then make my way over to my table.

The table is round with ten seats. It has been set up beautifully; Crisp white table cloths, more cutlery and glasses than anyone needs for one meal surely? And a beautiful centerpiece of white and blue lilies. I find my name card *Mrs. Blackford,* the card to the left of mine reads *Commissioner Blackford.*

I look around the table and see lots of names I don't recognize. I know that they are all senior members of the force though. I had better be on my best behavior tonight. Maybe limit myself to one or two glasses of wine. There is a little makeshift stage to my left. A tiny woman with crazy hair and little red half-moon specs climbs up onto the stage and goes over to the microphone.

"Ladies and Gentlemen, if you would please make your way to your seats, Mr. Turner will be making his opening speech in five minutes and then we can all finally eat!"

Everyone starts walking towards their seats and I see Kevin walking over with some portly looking old men and their partners. I stand up as they approach the table.

"Gentlemen I'd like you to meet my beautiful better half Rachel."

They all offer their hands to me and one by one Kevin introduces me.

"This is James, he is the Chief Constable, and his wife Linda. This is David, you know David, and his wife Simone. And this is Charles. Charles has just retired, he was the previous Commissioner and put my name in for the election without me even knowing!"

"Well I saw part of me in you and knew you were the right man for the job. Plus I was desperate to start my retirement and would have let anyone try for the job." He winks at Kevin as everyone laughs.

"And this is his wife Melissa."

"Mel please, lovely to meet you Rachel." She says. As she is shaking my hand, rather over enthusiastically, I notice her finger sparkling with the biggest diamond I have ever seen.

I'm shocked to say the least. I thought Mel was the commissioner's daughter! He is at least sixty, and she barely looks twenty.

"Lovely to meet you too Mel."

We all sit down as a waiter comes over and pours us all a glass of champagne. Another few men sit down and I smile and be polite. I have no idea or interest who they are if I'm being honest. These things bore me to death. If this Mr. Turner could get his rear end into gear and make his speech so I can eat and go home that would be wonderful. All the men at the table are discussing work, budgets, cases, it's all very boring. The wives must already know each other as they are deep in conversation about where they are going on holiday next year. I go to pick up my champagne and without even thinking I drain the glass. Well that was glass number two, maybe I will just have one more. Without me even having to look around, a very attentive waiter is already re filling my glass. He smiles as he walks away.

Everyone is seated and it's been almost fifteen minutes since the little crazy looking lady said that Mr. Turner would be five minutes. The crowd is starting to get impatient when I see her rushing over to the stage again.

"Apologies for the delay Ladies and Gents, but those of you that know Mr. Tuner as well as I do know he will probably be late for his own funeral."

The crowd all laughs.

Yes ha-ha now get on with it.

My stomach is growling angrily at me under the table.

"And without further delay I would like to introduce Thaddeus Turner."

The crowd starts to clap.

Thaddeus? What a coincidence, I have never heard anyone called Thaddeus in my life and then two in one day. I laugh to myself that they must be like busses. I join in clapping and then freeze on the spot when I see the gorgeous blue eyed Tad from the coffee shop this morning, stood at the microphone. His hair has been cut, it's shorter on the sides and long and styled at the top. His stubble has been trimmed to just barely there. He is wearing a grey tux, with a black bow tie and a white shirt. He looks breathtakingly hot. His deep blue eyes are staring straight into mine.

Shit. I think I've left a puddle on the chair. My stomach is in knots and I'm very aware of the heat coming from in between my legs. I have never in my life been this attracted to anyone. Ever.

He clears his throat and looks over the notes in his hand as the applause dies down.

"Good evening Ladies and Gentlemen. Apologies for keeping you all waiting, and yes I had already written that into my speech as anyone who knows me knows timekeeping is not my strong point!"

He pauses and the room erupts into loud laughter.

I'm so confused. Who is this guy?

"Welcome to tonight's annual fundraiser for the Police Dependents Trust. As most of you know this charity is one very close to my heart. My father was a police officer in London for almost twenty five years. As a boy, I looked up to him so much, I always wanted to follow in his footsteps, as did my brother Seb."

His voice breaks and he looks down and takes a sip of water. Charles leans over to Kevin and whispers

"I don't know if you heard but Sebastian Turner passed away suddenly about six weeks ago."

That must be Tad's brother. That must have been why he looked so incredibly sad this morning. Oh god, the urge to get up on stage to hug him is overwhelming. He manages to compose himself and carries on.

"However, it became apparent I didn't quite have what it took when Dad would find me laying on the floor struggling to breathe thirty seconds into our training sessions!" He pauses again to take a sip from his glass as everyone in the room laughs quietly.

"When I was twenty two, and Seb was just eighteen, we got a phone call that would change our lives. Dad had been killed on duty. An armed robbery had gone wrong and my Dad had been shot. As you can imagine we were all heartbroken. A week or so later a lady from the Police Dependents Trust got in touch with my mother. She talked us through all of the help and support that was available to us. Everything from supporting my mother financially so we didn't lose our house, to organizing bereavement counselling. I met so many people from that charity and I will forever be grateful to them for not only helping us all come to terms with what happened and helping us to deal with it. But for also helping out my mother, who would not have been able to afford to keep our house if it weren't for the charity. I vowed then that I would one day repay this charity for all they did for my family and me. Two years later after I sold off my first business, I donated two million pounds to the charity as thanks, and became a patron."

Two million pounds? Who the hell has two million pounds just laying around spare that he can give to charity? Jesus he must be rich.

"So for tonight, please eat and drink, then drink some more and place very large bids at the silent auction at the back of the room! I will leave you all to your food now. Please enjoy your night. Thank you."

The room erupts with applause and everyone stands as he exits the stage. Straight to our table. Oh fuck how can this be happening?!

CHAPTER EIGHT

Tad

The applause is dying down into loud chatter and the previous Commissioner, Charles, is introducing me to everyone seated at the table. I literally couldn't care less about most of them, there is only one person I care about meeting, again.

Eventually after a load of pointless chit chat we get to newly appointed Police and Crime Commissioner Kevin Blackford and his wife Rachel.

Definitely, definitely not dead then.

Damn.

"Commissioner Blackford, it's very nice to meet you, and congratulations on the new job."

I extend my hand, better be polite I suppose. He takes my hand and shakes it.

"Please call me Kevin, it's great to meet you. This is my wife Rachel."

Yes I know, I met her this morning and wanted to bang her brains out over the table in the middle of Costa.

I hold out my hand.

"Very nice to meet you Rachel."

She takes my hand and I swear a bolt of electricity travels through her and straight to my groin. I look up at her face, her eyes are staring into mine and she is biting her lip again. She really needs to stop doing that.

"It's lovely to meet you too Mr. Turner."

"Please, call me Tad."

I find my seat, I'm opposite Rachel. I pick up my name card and wander over to the man seated next to Rachel. I see his name is David.

"David, I wonder if there is any chance I could swap seats with you. I'm due to make another speech at the end of the meal and could do with being next to the stage."

What am I doing? Why am I chasing this girl? Not only is she married, but her husband is sitting right next to her.

David makes some stupid comment about being grateful for getting away from his wife and the girly chatter and then walks around to the other side of the table.

Rachel is holding her champagne flute and playing with the stem of the glass with her fingers. Oh fuck, I can't help but imagine it's my cock that she is playing with instead...

Calm yourself down. She is off limits.

I take my seat and she turns to look at me. Her cheeks are completely flushed, and her eyes look slightly glazed over, like she's turned on. No, not turned on, probably just had too much to drink. Stop looking for things that aren't there.

"Rachel." I say smiling at her.

"Tad." She is smiling back at me.

I sit down and an awkward silence crosses us both.

I can see her fidgeting nervously with her hands in her lap.

"Before I realised it was you giving the speech I thought that Thaddeus' were like busses." She blurts out.

"Huh?"

She suddenly looks embarrassed.

"You know like busses, don't see one for ages and then two come along at once. Because I didn't realise it was you giving the speech... So thought..." She puts her face in her hands and starts laughing.

"Ok ignore that, I'm sure I can come up with something more intelligent and less stupid. I blame the free champagne." She says as her cheeks blush an intense pink.

I laugh, she really is funny.

She looks back up at me, and we say nothing. The tension is so thick between us that it feels like everyone must be able to see it. Our eyes lock for a split second longer than is socially acceptable for two people who are supposed to be perfect strangers, and she quickly turns her head back around to her husband.

Yes, her husband.

The waiter is serving us some sort of fancy pants salad. I call it a salad, but it's essentially a few different types of lettuce leaves spread out across a huge plate with a couple of slices of duck and such a miniscule amount of sauce they might as well not have bothered putting any on the plate. I'm sure this is posh and someone would pay a load of money for it in a fancy restaurant but I'm far more of a burger and chips guy myself. But this is why I leave the food planning for these things to Suze. She seems to know what everyone else likes.

Everyone around the table starts to eat and is commenting on how nice the 'salad' is.

Rachel

After my stupid comment about busses I've hardly said two words. I'm just pretending to listen. I look concerned when everyone else does, and laugh on cue. My brain is currently residing in my knickers and there seems to be nothing I can do about it. Here I am, by some cruel twist of fate, sandwiched in between my husband, and this gorgeous sexy guy, who is making me extremely self-conscious about a potential wet patch on the seat when I stand up. Tad has been almost as quiet as me through the meal. Mel starts chatting to him from across the table.

"So how is it that you are here alone tonight then Thaddus?"

I snigger behind my wine glass, and feel a foot on my shin. I look up to see Tad stifling a laugh.

"It's Thaddeus, but please call me Tad."

Mel's cheeks flush red. She tilts her head to the side and licks her lips. What a slag, her husband is sitting next to her!

Pot kettle much?

"Ok Tad, how comes you are here alone tonight?"

"Well I was in a hurry and had to come on my motor bike, which only seats me." He says it so matter of factly that I can't help but burst out laughing. He looks at me and grins. God he is sexy. Kevin shoots me an evil look from my other side.

"Oh so have you left your girlfriend at home?"

"Yes I'd assume she is at home. In her home. Not that I would know where that is as I haven't met her yet." He smiles at Mel and takes a sip of his wine.

"Ah so you are single then?" Mel's eyes widen as if she is concocting a plan. "I have a friend who you would absolutely adore, you should let me set you up?"

"I'm not really looking for anyone at the moment but thanks very much for thinking of me. I'll let you know if I change my mind any time soon though."

"Ah shame, she is somewhere around here, if I see her I will bring her over, you know, just so you can be sure."

I can see Tad inwardly sighing. He lifts his glass at her and turns around and looks me in the eye.

"Please say you have something more exciting to talk about that police budgets, cafeteria food, Botox in your arse or blind dates?"

"Botox in your arse? Why on earth would anyone do that?!"

"You're asking me this? The second I heard what they were talking about I shut my ears off!"

A waiter comes over and Kevin loudly orders all the men at the table double vodka on the rocks. I suddenly look over to see three empty glasses in front of him already and realise that he is half shouting and slurring his words.

"Kevin?" I whisper to him.

He turns around sharply to look at me, his eyes don't quite catch up with him and I can see he is well on his way to being completely trashed. He is in front of important people he works with, he is going to make a complete idiot out of himself. Why does this man never know when he needs to stop?

"What?"

The smell of alcohol on his breath is enough to make me drunk myself.

"Umm, don't you think you should maybe slow down a bit?"

"What you on about? I'm fine?" He slurs

"It's just you're getting a bit loud and slurring a bit. Wouldn't want you getting pissed in front of people you work with?" I smile to try to make light of this. The last thing I want to do is piss him off.

I can see that David is shooting us a look, so I smile at him and he turns away.

Kevin looks down and when he looks back up I can see complete fury in his eyes. He is staring at me and he looks like he wants to kill me. He grabs my wrist under the table and squeezes hard. He leans in as if he is pretending to whisper sweet nothings in my ear.

"If I want your opinion Rachel I will ask for it."

He moves his face a centimeter from my own and stares at me.

"Got it."

He leans in closer and kisses me on the lips. I can feel my body flinch as his cold lips touch mine.

He pulls back and I just nod. He lets go of my wrist and he has left the imprint of his hand around it. I feel tears sting in my eyes, but there is not a chance I am going to cry here. I take a deep breath and turn back to the table with my wonderfully practiced fake smile. Tad is staring at me looking concerned.

"What was all that about?"

"Oh nothing," I lie "he has just had a bit too much."

I force out a half laugh and Tad smiles at me, still looking overly concerned. Why is he looking at me like that?

Without warning Kevin stands abruptly and tells me we are going.

"I've just seen the time, if you don't mind gentlemen I have a room upstairs and I want to make sure my wife and I make the most of it, if you know what I mean?"

He over exaggerates a wink at the men at the table and they all start laughing.

A room? He didn't tell me anything about staying here tonight? That means I have to spend all night in the same room as him. Fuck, in the same bed as him. When he is in this state and this angry at me? My horror must be apparent as Tad puts his hand on my shoulder and asks me again if I'm ok.

No I'm not, please don't make me spend the night alone with this drunken monster who just so happens to be the man I agreed to spend the rest of my life with.

"Yes honestly I am fine." I lie through a smile.

Kevin sees Tad's hand on my shoulder and painfully grabs me under the arm as he pulls me up off the chair. He glares at Tad and then grabs my arm and yanks me away.

I can't help it now, the tears are coming and I can't stop them. I will myself to just get past the people in the room.

I manage to hold my composure until we get through the doors, then the tears start streaming. I am utterly terrified about what is going to happen once we are locked in a room together.

"What the fuck are you crying for?"

"You're hurting me Kevin!"

I'm desperately trying to keep as calm as possible but I can feel I am on the verge of a meltdown.

"Hurting you? You haven't seen anything yet Rachel. I don't know who the fuck you think you are, but I think you need to remember you are my fucking *wife*."

We walk through a second set of doors and he throws me down a small corridor leading to the toilets. Before I know what is happening he has me pinned up against the wall. One hand around my throat, pushing me back and the other holding the wall next to my hip.

"I don't know what I've done Kevin. Please get off of me!" I'm struggling to breathe as his hand is pressing against my throat. This is the most awful moment of my life.

"I've seen those eyes before, those eyes you were giving Mr. fucking millionaire. Those 'please fuck me eyes'. You've only ever looked at me like that once before, but I remember what it looks like, and you were looking at him like that."

He is talking at me through gritted teeth and I can feel his spit spraying my face. The smell of alcohol coming off of him is making me feel sick.

"Kevin I swear I wasn't looking at him anyway. I was just making polite conversation."

"Do you think I'm fucking stupid?"

He starts to move his hand from the wall onto my hip. My eyes widen as I realise what he is about to do, I feel like I'm about to throw up.

"Kevin, please stop! Let me go!"

His hand moves under the slit in my dress and over my leg. He touches my underwear and then I start to feel him getting hard through his trousers.

"You filthy little whore! You're dripping wet. Well it seems a shame to waste this."

His eyes suddenly flash, in a second he goes from furiously angry to excited.

I start shaking uncontrollably, and my brain starts screaming at me that I need to get out of here. Get away from him.

The next thing I know Kevin is being dragged away from me and I slide down the wall into a heap on the floor. Tad has appeared out of nowhere and is wrestling with Kevin in the middle of the hallway. I must be having some sort of nightmare. None of this seems real. Suddenly two big burly men in black suits come running up to Kevin and each grabs an arm. He is flailing his arms like a man possessed trying to escape. One arm becomes free and he makes a swing for Tad.

"You keep away from my fucking wife!" He is yelling and screaming, and a few people walking past turn their heads to see what the noise is.

One of the men in the suits punches Kevin straight in the nose and he falls to the floor unconscious. The three men all look over to me. Without a thought I get up and run into the ladies and lock myself in a cubicle.

What the hell just happened? Things went from a nice civilized night out, to my own husband assaulting me and then getting knocked out.

A few minutes pass and I'm sat on the toilet with the lid down, head in my hands when I hear the door open.

"Rachel?"

Shit, it's Tad.

"Yeah, um I'm fine."

"Can you come out here a minute?"

"No really I'm ok thanks, I'm just calling a cab."

Shit, where is my bag?

"Well that seems unlikely seeing as I have your bag."

Busted. I can hear the kindness in his voice. I stand up, wipe under my eyes to try to wipe away any mascara streaks, straighten my dress and open the door.

When I open the door he looks up from the floor and smiles at me. He is leaning up against the sinks. His bow tie is undone and his top button is open. I smile weakly back at him and walk over to the mirror. Amazingly my waterproof make up has stayed pretty much intact. You'd never know I'd just had a fight with my husband, well apart from the bright red finger prints around my throat. I take out the hair pins from my chignon and let me hair down. I shake it out gently and it covers most of the marks on my neck. No awkward stares or questions now.

I turn to grab my bag from Tad and he is just staring at me with his mouth slightly open. I stand looking at him staring for what feels like ages when he suddenly gives himself a little shake and passes me my bag. I open it up to grab my phone, and - Fuck. What a bastard.

"He has taken my phone out. And my bank card, and my keys."

"Why would he do that?"

Tad looks concerned again. He gets these sexy little frown lines when he looks at me all concerned like that.

Stop it, this is what got you in this mess in the first place.

"Just too much to drink I guess. He isn't normally like that." I lie.

Tad says nothing but gives me a look like he sees right through me.

He shakes his head.

"You have a room here tonight though anyway, so at least you're sorted for tonight."

"Oh no, I need to get home. I don't want to spend any time alone with him. I mean, he just needs time to sober up that's all."

"He was escorted out of the hotel by security and put in a cab, don't worry about him for tonight."

I can't help but be worried that Kevin's boss might find out about all of this and he might get in trouble. Or lose his new job. Then life at home would be unbearable.

Life at home is already unbearable and you really need to get some balls and find a way out of this.

I smile at Tad.

"Thank you. I guess I will go and get a key to my room and head up."

"Umm... Would you like to have a drink with me at the bar? Just so I can make sure you are ok?"

I know I should say no, my head is a mess. But the thought of a huge glass of wine is very appealing. But sitting next to Tad, alone, when I'm feeling this vulnerable is probably not a good idea.

Just go to bed before you get yourself in anymore trouble woman.

"A drink would be great" I smile at him as the sensible voice in my head sighs and disappears back into the corner of my brain not used much.

"Go and wait for me at the bar, I will be there in two minutes. Just have to thank everyone for coming."

He holds the door open for me and points over to the direction of the bar.

CHAPTER NINE

Tad

I have no idea how she has managed to stay so calm and collected throughout this evening. Her 'husband' has treated her like dirt since his third or fourth drink. I can't work out if she didn't notice all of his dirty looks in her direction and all of the disgusting little comments he made about her, or if she is so used to them that they don't even affect her anymore. The latter mates my heart hurt. This beautiful, funny, intelligent creature should be absolutely worshipped. How the hell did she end up with a monster like that?

I walk over to the bar and I can see her fiddling with her fingers and looking down at the floor. She looks really nervous. I'm nervous. Over and over I hear myself say *she is married. She is married.* But she is married to an evil prick of a man.

But she is still married, her husband has just attacked her and she is clearly shaken.

I need to make sure I act like more of a man than that thing she is married to; even if all I want to do is carry her up to my suite, rip her clothes off of her and fuck her until the sun comes up.

She looks up at me as I walk towards her and smiles at me.

"What would you like to drink?" Every time she looks me in the eyes I can't help but smile at her.

"I can't decide between being sensible and just having a glass of wine or having a dozen shots and forgetting this dreadful night." She chuckles, and it looks like she is genuinely feeling better.

The barman is waiting for our order.

"Can I have a bottle of your nicest white wine, a bottle of your smoothest vodka and two shot glasses please? We will be sitting over there. Please charge it to my account, I'm Mr. Turner in The Blue."

I catch Rachel grinning next to me.

I give him a £50 tip and walk over to a secluded table in the corner of the room.

I pull out a chair and offer it to Rachel, she smiles at me and sits down.

"You really are a gentleman aren't you?"

"Well not really; but I do know how to treat women with respect." I'm smiling but see her face fall. She looks down at the table. Shit, she probably thinks I'm having a dig at her about her idiot husband.

"Shit. I didn't mean anything by that Rachel. Sorry."

She looks up from the table at me with glistening eyes.

"You must think I'm an idiot." She whispers as a tear escapes her eye and rolls down her cheek.

"Oh God no Rachel, of course I don't!" Without thinking I reach across the table and grab her hands in mine. There it is again, that electricity every time we touch. "I do wonder why on earth you are with him though."

At that moment the guy from the bar brings over a tray with our drinks. She snatches her hands quickly away and wipes her face. He starts to pour out our wine and I'm silently willing him to hurry the hell up.

When he finishes, I pour us both a shot of vodka. Rachel swallows it in one. I follow suit. It burns the back of my throat slightly as it goes down.

She puts her glass down and I push her wine glass towards her.

"He hasn't ever done anything like that before." She looks up at me and it's glaringly obvious she is lying.

"Why don't I believe you?"

She throws a defensive look my way and takes a deep breath in as if she is about to argue with me. Then she exhales and drops her shoulders, looking defeated.

"Maybe because I have always been a bad liar?"

I stay silent and take a sip of my wine, hoping that she will tell me more without me having to pry too much.

"He hasn't always been like this though. He used to be lovely."

"How long have you been together?"

"We met eleven years ago, we've been married for nine years now." She is looking down at the table, almost as if she is slightly embarrassed. She doesn't look old enough to have been with someone for that long.

"Eleven years? Did you meet him when you were ten?" I smile at her and try to lighten the mood a little. It works and she looks at me with a smile.

"I was sixteen when we met. He was twenty five."

What a pervert.

"How come you got married so young?"

She starts shuffling about in her seat.

"Well it seemed... appropriate..."

"Appropriate?"

"We were married three months after I had my daughter." She takes a long gulp of her wine.

She has a daughter? And she is married, to a pervert psycho. What am I doing here? I don't need this shit in my life, my life is complicated enough without falling for someone with this amount of emotional baggage. I look across and see Rachel staring at me. Waiting for me to say something.

"Wow."

It's all I can think to say.

Rachel

I can't for the life of me work out what he is thinking.

"She is the best thing that has ever happened to me, and I wouldn't change her for the world. I know I was young when I had her but she is my absolute life, and if I had to start my life over, even with the knowledge of what her father would put me through, I would still do everything the same as I could never be without her."

He smiles at me and takes a sip of his wine.

"So when did things get bad?" He looks so intense.

"To be honest, it wasn't all that long after we were married. Just small things at first. Like if I wanted to go out with my friends, he would make some comment about it so I wouldn't go. Or he would throw food away that I had bought because he didn't want me getting fat. He once threw away a load of my clothes as he thought they were too revealing. Oh and one time he messaged all my friends from my phone number saying awful things to them and then blocked their numbers without my knowledge..." I can't believe I am opening up to him like this. The only other person that knows all of this is Celine, and even then I have watered down some of it as I was simply too ashamed. I just feel like I can tell Tad anything. I don't know what this connection is, I've never felt anything like it before.

He looks so sad as I speak.

"Rachel, that is awful. Why would you let him control you like that? You must have known it was wrong? Why on earth are you still with him when this has been going on for so long?" He has gone from looking sad to looking angry and it makes my eyes well up again. This is not me. I am a strong person. I don't cry over Kevin. What is going on with me?

"Shit Rachel, I'm sorry please don't cry." He stands up and walks over to my side and crouches down next to me. "I just can't understand why you would be with someone like him? You are intelligent, and funny, and beautiful! You could do so much better than him. Why stay?"

He has the kindest eyes I have seen. Something about him seems so genuine, so comfortable.

"I stay for Amelia. I tried to leave once, when Ami was about six months old. I had already taken her to my mums and left her there while I went home to pack some things. He came home and flipped out. Like totally lost it, I had never been so scared in all my life. He dragged me upstairs and locked me in the bedroom for hours. He came back in the evening with Ami, and a big envelope. He came into my room and threw the envelope at me and told me to open it. Inside was a needle and syringe, a small bag filled with white powder and a lump of something grey looking wrapped in cling film. He told me that if I ever tried to leave him again he would force all that shit in my body, leave me in some drug den for the police to find and would have social services remove Ami from me completely."

I have never seen anyone look so angry or so shocked all in one. Tears are spilling down my cheeks now and I just can't help it. I have never ever admitted that to anyone. Not even Celine knows. I have lived with the fear of what my own husband might one day do to me for so many years and now I have started to open up I can't seem to stop myself. What is it about this man that makes me trust him so much when I hardly know him?

Without a word, Tad stands, gently grabs my shoulders and pulls me up into his chest, he wraps his arms around me and it feels so right. I feel safe. I can hear his heart hammering against his chest. I can feel his breath in my hair. He smells gorgeous, I can't help but take a deep breath in. He smells like cologne, but it's strange. It's sweet but almost smells slightly like petrol. Whatever it is it is wonderful and I can't help but close my eyes as I take another deep breath in. I'm feeling totally overwhelmed, it can't be possible for one person to feel so many emotions at one time. The main one I am aware of though is lust. Pure, intense, sex clenching lust. I know I need to leave. I need to pull myself out of his big, strong, safe arms, get up to my room and forget about him.

So go then.

I pull away from his chest and look up at him.

Mistake.

I want him. I run my tongue along my bottom lip as I am staring at his, wondering what it would be like if he kissed me. I look up at his eyes and they look different. I have never seen anyone look at me like this, ever. Gone are those kind eyes from minutes ago, replaced by deep pools of desire. His eyes keep darting to my lips, then back to my eyes, he wants to kiss me.

Don't do it. Get upstairs and have a very cold shower, NOW, before you do something you will regret.

I trail my hand up his rock hard chest, he closes his eyes as a pained look crosses his face. My hand moves further up until I can feel his stubble under my fingers, I carry on and let my thumb gently brush his luscious lips. A low growl escapes his lips that makes my insides clench. His eyes shoot open and the next thing I know he is pulling me into him as his lips rush to find mine. It's desperate and frantic, as if he has been wanting to give in and kiss me since the second we met. His soft lips brush against my own, his stubble scratching my face, it is sensory overload. It feels so good. I part my lips to let his tongue find mine, our tongues dance around each other and his arms are stroking down my back until they reach my arse. His hands gently squeeze my cheeks and I can't help but moan softly. Fuck I want this man so much that it physically hurts. My sex is throbbing in between my legs and I know that if I wasn't wearing underwear I would be dripping down my leg. I can feel that he feels the same way by the growing bulge against my stomach, what I wouldn't give to be able to get on my knees and taste his beautiful cock.

After what feels like hours of standing, groping, kissing; a hideous thought crosses my mind. I am married and I am in a hotel where an event was just held where almost every guest knows my husband. What the hell am I doing? I quickly pull away from Tad.

"Fuck. I'm – I'm so sorry Tad."

I step backwards without looking and almost trip over my fucking chair. I need to get out of here.

"No, shit, I'm sorry. Rach, please don't go."

I've grabbed my bag and I'm already hurrying off to find the nearest lift. I can hear his footsteps behind me and I almost break into a run. I've got to get away from him.

"Tad just please, leave me alone." I call over my shoulder. And the footsteps stop.

I find a lift and hammer the button so hard I think it might break. What have I done? Why did I do that?

I told you to get out of there.

Tears are spilling out of my eyes once more and I can't wait any longer for this lift. I take off my shoes and go through the door to the left and climb the stairs to my floor instead.

CHAPTER TEN

Tad

Stupid, stupid, *stupid* man.

Why would you kiss her? She was scared and vulnerable and you took advantage of her. You absolute idiot.

I've come back to my room and raided the mini bar for, well, anything alcoholic at this point.

My suite is huge, and blue. Given the situation it suits my mood completely. It feels cold and empty. It's a beautiful room, but it's too big for one person. There are two sofas and two armchairs in the middle of the room. A glass coffee table stands in the middle of the two sofas. No matter where I sit, in front of me in an empty seat. It just seems to remind me that apart from my PA and my business partner, I don't really have anyone in my life anymore. And now, I meet a genuinely wonderful woman, who more than anything right now probably just needed a friend, and I have successfully ruined any chance of ever seeing her again.

I sit on the sofa and put my head in my hands. I should have pulled away, now she probably thinks I'm just as much of an arsehole as her husband.

That kiss though... I can't stop thinking about it. I know it shouldn't have happened, but it was incredible. Like no other kiss I have had in my life.

I get out my laptop and open up Facebook. I type "Rachel Blackford" into the search bar. There are a few results, but she is the top one and it turns out we have three friends in common. I open up her profile. It is pretty locked down, so all I can see are her profile and cover photos. Her profile picture is her. Just her, beautiful her. Hardly any make up, beautiful big blue eyes staring into the camera and her stunning smile. A strand of her silky brown hair is blowing across her face, and it reminds me of when I first saw her at the beach this morning. Her cover photo is of her with a little girl next to her, I assume that is her daughter, Amelia was it? She looks like a younger version of her mum, except she has blonde curls. I click on the message icon and sit for a while staring at the blinking cursor. I want to apologise, I want to tell her how amazing she is, and how incredible that kiss was. I want to tell her to leave that scum bag husband and that I will protect her and her daughter. I put my laptop on the table and go over to pour myself another drink instead. I've known this woman all of five minutes, and she has already had more of an impact on me than anyone else ever has.

Rachel

*H*e is standing at the end of my bed, licking his lips while he stares at me in my bed. I sit up and start to undress myself. I can see his cock harden from under his trousers. He runs a hand over his growing bulge, closes his eyes and groans, low and sexy.

I am naked. I lay on my back and open my legs in invitation. He kneels on the bed and crawls towards me, his eyes staring into mine.

"Oh what a beautiful pussy you have Rach. I want to taste it. Can I taste you baby?"

"Oh God! Yes Tad, please!" I beg.

Without warning he buries his face in between my legs, his tongue darts straight for my swollen clit and he starts circling his tongue around it. His stubble is scratching around me and I feel like I am about to come already. I run my fingers through his hair and push him harder into me. I am close. He can tell, so he pulls away. He moves lower, takes his tongue and thrusts it inside of me, he is licking me deep, tasting every inch of me. It feels amazing, I want his cock inside me, I need to feel him fill me up.

"Tad, please, fuck me!" I am practically begging.

"Not yet baby."

He moves his tongue back up to my clit and starts to suck on it, at the same time he pushes two fingers deep into me and works me hard from the inside. He is sucking and nibbling at my clit and pushing his fingers in and out of me in a frenzy.

"Rach, baby?" he mumbles with my clit still in his mouth.

"Yes Tad, yes." I can barely think, let alone speak.

"Come for me. Now."

Without warning, I come on his command. I come violently, my hips lifting off the bed and screams escaping my mouth.

I wake suddenly, sweat dripping from my face. I am soaking wet and throbbing. Tad isn't here, it was a dream. That orgasm however was very, *very* real. I haven't orgasmed like that in, well, ever. And that was only with the dream Tad.

I try to get back to sleep but end up tossing and turning for a few hours until its late enough to wake up. My head is pounding and I have this feeling of dread deep in the pit of my stomach. I'm convinced someone saw me last night and has told Kevin. Fuck.

What am I going to go home to?

I wander into the bathroom to look at the damage. A deep purple bruise is forming all around my throat, and it's not hard to see that it resembles a hand. And – Shit! I have fucking stubble rash all around my mouth. Images flash through my head of Tad grabbing my arse and snogging me out of my mind. What was I thinking?

Kevin packed a bag for us and must have had it sent here earlier in the day as it was in the room when I got here, he did pack clothes and shower stuff but he wouldn't have been able to pack my make up as I was using it last night before we left. Fuck! How am I going to cover this up? I start to cry again. This is ridiculous, I'm going to dehydrate at this rate, I've got to get a hold of myself. I need to hold my head up high, get home, and do some serious damage control.

CHAPTER ELEVEN

It's 7.30am. I am showered and dressed. I've attempted to blow-dry my hair around my neck so that it hides the bruise, but for now there is nothing I can do about the stubble rash. I go to take out my phone to check train times and then my stomach flips when I remember that bastard took my phone and my card. I have no money. I have no way of getting home. I am stranded in the middle of London. I will have to jump a train and hope to God that there are no ticket inspectors working today. What a fucking mess.

Suddenly there is a knock at my door and I freeze. My heart starts hammering away in my chest. Shit, what if it's Kevin?

Knock knock.

Shit! I tiptoe over to the door.

"Who is it?"

"Room service Ms. Blackford."

Room service? I didn't order any room service?

"I think you have the wrong room, I haven't ordered anything?"

"It is sent with compliments of Mr. Turner."

What? Why has Tad ordered me room service?

"Oh. Umm please pass along my thanks but I don't need anything. Thank you."

"Apologies Ms. Blackford, Mr. Turner said you would probably say that so he told me to leave it here for you. Enjoy."

And with that, I hear footsteps walking in the opposite direction, they get quieter and then nothing.

I open the door and peek though the crack. There is a trolley just outside my door loaded with coffee, tea, cereals, toast, a full English breakfast and a bottle of champagne. On the bottom shelf is a large Selfridge's bag. Intrigued, I pull the cart into my room, close the door and look inside the bag. It is filled with shower gel, body lotion, shampoo, and a load of designer make up. Underneath all of that is what looks like clothes. I tip the makeup and toiletries out on the floor and see two pairs of jeans, not just any jeans, but jeans with a £230 price tag! Who on earth would pay that much for jeans! There is a size 10 and a size 12, gosh he is hopeful! I don't remember the last time my hips and bum fit in a size 10 anything! There is a beautiful jumper underneath the jeans, it is oversized and grey with big white stars. £260?

What the hell? That is £720 alone on just clothes, let alone everything else. I look through the makeup, Tom Ford, Mac, Bobby Brown... I know for a fact this make up isn't exactly cheap and there is an entire collection there, primer, foundation, mascara, palettes, the lot. Some guy that I have only spoken to for one night and then drunkenly threw myself at has just spent over a grand on me. What is this? I can't help but be really pissed off. I guess he thinks this came from a good place but why? Pity?

Or maybe he likes you...

Next to a jug of orange juice there is an envelope with my name on it. I open it –

"Rachel,

It occurred to me that as you had no idea you were staying here and as things went so wrong with your husband that you probably didn't have any clothes etc. here, and as you are also without your phone or any money you wouldn't be able to sort anything out.

I really hope you don't mind, but I asked my assistant to run out early this morning to sort some bits out for you.

I thought you might be hungry too and wasn't sure what you liked so just ordered everything.

I'm so sorry about the way things ended last night. I really hope you are feeling ok.

I know the situation isn't great, but is there any chance we could meet up one day? I usually stay in London but I am from Chichester and have a house there so I am often around.

I just want to make sure you are ok.

Here is my number, please at least call or text me to let me know you are safe when you get home. I know I barely know you but for some reason I can't get you out of my mind, and I'm worried about you.

Tad

P.s. There is paracetamol and ibuprofen in the little paper bag, in case you feel as rough as I do."

His number is at the bottom of the note.

I re read *"For some reason I can't get you out of my mind"*. I know the feeling. I still don't know how to take this, but at least this way I can put a bit of make-up on to cover the bruising and stubble rash. I take out all of the make-up, I only open the foundation and the face powder. The rest can go back, I don't need any of the rest of it and while I appreciate the gesture, it is far too much. I pour myself a coffee and drain the cup, it's the most amazing coffee I've ever tasted I pour myself another and pick at some toast.

When I am finally ready I pack up the clothes and make up and put them back on the trolley. I pen my own note and place it in the bag. I gather my things and go to check out in reception.

"How was your stay Mrs. Blackford?" The pretty lady at reception asks me with a beaming smile.

"Yeah it was lovely." I lie. "The beds are so comfortable." That was true, and being awake half of the night meant I got even more time to appreciate just how comfy they were!

"Like seeping on a cloud!" She laughs. "So I can see your bill is all paid up, and if you would just wait a couple of minutes I will call your car to the front of the hotel?"

Huh? I guess that Kevin paid in advance for the hotel, but my car? Did Kevin arrange for a cab to take us home too?

"What car is that?"

"Your friend Mr. Turner arranged for a private car to take you back to Chichester this morning." She chirps at me.

This man... I don't know how I should feel about this but I'm too tired and anxious to get home to do anything so I just smile.

"Speaking of my friend Mr. Turner, he had some things sent to my room but I didn't need them. I have left them in a bag in my room, could you please make sure he gets them back?"

"Of course Mrs. Blackford. If you just take a seat your car will be here in a couple of minutes."

I thank her and take a seat on one of the plush sofas in the reception area.

CHAPTER TWELVE

Tad

I am on my fifth cup of coffee and I'm trying my hardest to concentrate and think of anything other than Rachel. I am so worried about her. If her husband could treat her like that in a public place then who knows what the hell he might do to her at home. I slam the lid of my laptop down in frustration. I am supposed to be preparing for an important meeting on Monday. Scott has been trying to get this meeting for months, and has finally worn the company down and they are willing to discuss us buying them out. This kind of thing normally excites me. The prospect of buying some failing company, turning it all around and then selling it off for a shit load more than I paid for it. It's what I thrive on. I'm normally up for nights before important meetings like this one, doing as much research as I possibly can. Doing the sums to work out how many of the staff I can keep on, and how I can keep as many of them as safe as possible in their jobs, even once I've sold the company on. I was up all night last night, but as hard as I tried to start writing a plan of action, or do some research on the company and the bosses, I just could not get Rachel out of my mind. The way she looked up at me, her eyes silently pleading with me to kiss her. At least that's what I felt. And she kissed me back, she must have wanted it to. Nobody kisses like that unless they really want it. I can feel my boxers getting tighter just by thinking about kissing her. This is hell.

I always used to believe in fate before Seb died. It's almost as if she has been thrown at me to try to prove to me that everything that happens is supposed to and for a good reason. Except of course that she is already fucking married. I bury my face in my hands and try to talk myself into focusing on the task at hand.

Just then the phone stats to ring. I walk over to the desk and answer it.

"Hello?"

"Good morning Mr. Turner. Just to let you know as requested that Mrs. Blackford has just arrived back at her house in Chichester."

"Brilliant, thank you for letting me know."

"Also Sir, she left a bag for you in her room. Would you like me to bring it up to you, or should I leave it behind the reception desk for you?"

A bag?

Surely she isn't stubborn enough to have gone home wearing her dress from last night?

"Could you bring it up to me please?"

"Of course Sir, it will be up with you in a moment."

"Thank you."

I hang up and scratch my head in confusion, why wouldn't she just accept what I bought for her as a gift? It would have made her life easier, and I wasn't sure what to get so I told Suze just to get everything.

A couple of minutes later and someone from reception has bought the bag up for me. Poking out of the top of the bag is a letter.

"*Tad,*

OK so at first I was pissed off that you bought all this stuff for me. I hardly know you and then threw myself at you, and had no idea what this was. But then I read your letter and actually just think you're a really nice guy. Far too nice if I'm honest. Anyway I didn't need any clothes as I had things here, and I have a whole load of toiletries and make up at home, so it didn't seem right to keep everything. I did use a bit of the makeup but will happily pay you back for it.

I don't think that meeting up is a good idea. I am married, and I kissed you. I shouldn't have done that, and in all honesty I can't guarantee it wouldn't happen again if we were to meet. You seem like an amazing man and don't need my drama in your life. Please don't worry about me. I have been looking after myself for years, I will be fine.

Thank you for everything, just listening to me ramble on judgement free meant more to me than you could ever know.

In another life Tad I would have said this was fate...

Rachel xxx"

What does she mean by that? Oh God what has this woman done to me. The thought of not seeing her again makes me feel sick.

I am supposed to be staying in London for this meeting Monday but if I stay here I will go crazy. Maybe I already am crazy. I get out my phone and call Scott.

"Hey bud, how was your police thing last night?"

"Hey Scott, it was, um, interesting." Scott is my business partner but also my best friend, yet I have no idea what to say to him.

I stopped a man beating the shit out of his wife then I snogged her and now I think that she is my long lost soul mate?

"Interesting eh? Is that code for I got my dick wet?" He laughs at me.

"Uh, no. Listen Scott, I know you have been on at Serenity for ages and have just managed to get this meeting but do you think you would be ok to handle it on your own?"

"Tad, what's happened?" In a breath, all joking has stopped and he sounds deadly serious.

"Nothing. Nothing, I just have a lot on my mind at the moment, and I think maybe I should take a bit of time off. I know you can handle everything for a few days."

"This isn't like you man, I'm worried about you. But I do agree you need some time off. You've worked nonstop for months, even with everything with Seb."

I hear his voice crack slightly, he and Seb were close. We all were.

I sigh down the phone.

"Just a few days Scott, I just need to get my head in a better place."

"Yeah man no problem. Promise me you will call if you need anything yeah?"

"Of course, you know me."

"Yeah I do, which is why I'm worried! Don't worry about Serenity. It's been me badgering Harris for this meeting anyway so I'm already all up to speed."

"Cheers mate, give me a call tomorrow if you want to run through anything, otherwise give me a call or drop me an e-mail on Monday to let me know how it went."

"Ok buddy, speak to you soon. And I mean it, you need anything just call."

"Thanks Scott, speak soon."

I've known Scott for years now, and he is genuinely one of the nicest guys I've ever met.

Now I need to figure out what the hell I am doing with my life.

CHAPTER THIRTEEN

Rachel

I am standing outside of my front door terrified to open it. I checked my make up at least ten times in the car. He is going to take one look at me and know, that is if someone hasn't already told him. How the hell have I got myself into this mess?

I take a deep breath and ring the doorbell.

No answer.

I knock.

No answer.

I try the door handle and it is unlocked. Normally it's always locked, whether we are in or out, so this is strange. I open the door and peek my head round.

"Kevin?"

I can't hear anything at all, I don't think he is in. I walk through the door and put my bag down. I walk through the hallway and into my front room and stop dead in my tracks. The room has been completely trashed. Every book from my book case has been torn up and thrown around the room, the armchair is on its side with the cushions scattered throughout the room, and the glass coffee table has been smashed. I am suddenly terrified that someone has broken into the house. Shit what if they are still here. I walk into the kitchen and see that all of the plates and glasses that were in the draining board have been smashed on the floor. On the side next to the sink is my phone, keys and bank card. My car key is there and my car is out of the front. There is no way someone broke in and made this mess or they would have taken my car, or at least my phone. No, this is all Kevin. My fear turns to anger and it takes a lot to not scream.

I hear a noise coming from the utility room next door. It sounds like the washing machine? I peek my head round and sure enough there is a load in the machine about to have its final spin. Out of all the things wrong in my house right now, this is the one that screams the loudest to me. In the nine years we have lived together, I think Kevin has put a wash on about three times. I have no idea what could be so important he would need to wash it in the middle of trashing our house? It's not like I've never seen his shirts covered in makeup, or stinking of perfume, or even seen white crusty stains all over his boxers. He has never ever cared about me seeing that stuff before, why now?

I go back into the kitchen, pull out a chair from under the table and sit down. I sob. I haven't cried this much in years. This is it, this is my life. If I could just be brave and leave here, then I could be with someone like Tad. Someone who touches me and makes everything feel right, someone whose kisses send me to places I have never been. But I am not brave. I am a coward, and I am scared. Scared of having the one good thing in my life taken away from me, and scared of what might happen to her if she had to live with her dad full time.

I wipe my eyes and go to my phone. It is on charge so he was obviously going through it last night. I'm not entirely sure what he expects to find on there?

I search for my mum and dads number and call them.

"Hello?"

"Hi Daddy." I smile, I have the best Dad in the world. He is the only person in my family who sees through some of Kevin's bullshit.

"Hello princess, how are you doing?"

"I'm good thanks, how are you? Hope Ami isn't wearing you out too much?"

"We are good, she is definitely keeping us on our toes though! I haven't been up at six for years!"

"Is that Mum?" I hear a little excited voice talking to my Dad. He passes the phone over to her.

"Mummy!! I am having such an amazing time. I spoke to the boy who lives next door yesterday Mummy, his name is Theo, he is really nice, he just moved here and is going to be starting in my school at the start of term, he is ten though so he is older than me, but he is really nice, he showed me where to find the best Pokémon." I hear her take a long breath and can't help but giggle to myself.

"Sounds like you're having a great time! So is Theo your boyfriend then?" I tease.

"Mum! Don't be so silly! Of course he is not my *boyfriend*!"

"Ok ok! I was just asking! So apart from Pokémon hunting with the neighbour have you been up to anything else?"

"Nanny and Gramps bought a caravan!"

"They did what?!"

"Yeah, we went to look at them, and one of them was really cool, and the sofa turns into a bed, and it has a shower over the toilet and it's really awesome. I'm helping nanny decorate it." I can hear how happy she is and it makes me feel like my troubles have faded away.

"Gramps wants to talk to you again Mummy, but I will send you a photo of the caravan later, it's awesome. Love you loads Mummy, bye"

"Love you baby."

I hear her pass the phone back to my dad.

"Rachel did you have any plans for this week?"

"I do have a few things I need to get done, why?"

"Well your mum and I wanted to give the caravan a test run, so thought about going to the Isle of Wight for a few days, and we wondered if you and Ami wanted to come with us?"

A few days away from Kevin, away from everything that has happened would do me good. But if I go away I won't be able to accidentally bump into Tad...

Which is all the more reason to go, surely?

"Oh Dad I'd love to, but I have a couple of things planned that I can't really get out of." Why did I say that? Why do the sensible things my brain suggests just get pushed out of the way for stupid things that are just going to get me in trouble?

"Oh that's a shame. It was Ami's idea really, she was really looking forward to it."

"Well take Ami for a few days, if you want to?" I hate being away from her but to be honest I really need to sort myself out before she comes home, and see what is going on with Kevin.

"Well we can get the ferry tomorrow morning, and come back Friday so she would be gone all week. Is that ok?"

A whole week without her and without her being just down the road. God I will miss her, but I know she will really enjoy it, and I will talk to her all the time. This is one of the reasons I got her a phone. For emergencies, and I always count as an emergency.

"As long as it is ok with you guys then its fine with me. Do you have enough clothes and things at yours or do you want me to drop some things round?

"You know what your mum is like princess, Ami has enough clothes here to last until she is eighteen."

"Gramps come on lets go, tell mum to call later!" I can hear Ami getting impatient in the background and I laugh to myself.

"It sounds like you're needed Dad! I will call you later okay?"

"Speak later princess, I love you."

"Love you too Dad."

I put my phone down on the table, stand up and go towards the front room, I had better start tidying up this mess.

I go to walk through the kitchen door and standing there is Kevin. He startles me so much that I jump backwards, hard into the corner of the table. Ouch! That fucking hurts. I'm clutching at my hip trying to stop the pain, and at the same time I am trying to look at his face, looking for any signs that he knows.

We just stand staring at each other for a long few seconds. I have no idea what to say to him.

Finally he breaks the silence.

"You didn't come home." His voice is hoarse. He looks a mess. His hair is all over the place, and his eyes are completely bloodshot. There is a bruise starting to form around his nose and left eye.

Good, I hope that fucking hurt.

"You didn't give me much choice. You took my money, phone and keys. What was I supposed to do? Walk the entire way home?" I reply curtly.

"Did you fuck him?" His eyes are burning into me. I am so shocked I just open my mouth and stare at him. Shit, does he know about the kiss?

"What are you talking about?" I try to stay as calm as possible, but the wobble of my voice betrays me. He takes a step towards me.

"You were gushing over him all night, we fight and then you don't come home. I am asking you if you stayed behind to fuck him."

I don't think he knows about the kiss. I straighten my back a little and try to look like I am not an absolute wreck inside.

"Of course I didn't fuck him Kevin. I am not like you." His lips start to curl into a smirk.

I hear my phone buzz on the table and we both look over to it. It is probably just Ami texting me, but my heart is hammering away. Kevin looks back towards me and then walks over to my phone. He picks it up, swipes the screen and starts putting in my long over complicated password. How the hell did he work that out? It is a combination of mine, and Ami's names, with our birthdays thrown in and a couple of random full stops. There is no way he guessed that...

"Message request from Thaddeus Turner..." He reads out loud and I stop breathing. What do I do? What if Tad mentions us kissing in his message? Why the fuck would he message me? He knows exactly what Kevin is like and he must know I am home by now. Oh god. I could lunge at him, grab the phone and make a run for the front door? But Kevin goes to the gym two times most days, he is built like a brick house, there is no way I would be able to get past him. I can't breathe, I can't move. I am stood paralysed to the spot. Kevin reads the message and I see his face fill with rage.

"I know you said not to worry but I can't help it," he reads out, "please just let me know you got home safely and then I won't bother you again."

I can breathe again, thank God for that. I look up at Kevin but see that his face has gone bright red and he looks furious.

He takes two long strides towards me and pushes me back into the counter.

"Why the fuck is this prick messaging you?" He hisses at me. His breath still reeks of alcohol and I wonder when he last had a drink? He probably isn't anywhere near sober yet. What was I doing coming home? I should have left him to sober up for the day and came back later.

I feel my stomach drop, and my heart starts to hammer so loudly in my chest he must be able to hear it.

"ANSWER ME!" He screams in my face. He puts his hands either side of me and rests them on the counter so his face is only centimeters away from my own.

"I don't know Kevin! He checked I was ok last night after you decided to act like a monster at the hotel, and then I went up to my room. That is it. He is probably just checking that you didn't kill me the second I walked through the door!" I shout back at him. He stands up, and starts to turn around to walk out. He throws my phone at me.

"Prick..." I mutter under my breath.

Why did you say that, you absolute idiot!

Without warning he spins around on his heels and pulls his left hand behind him, the next thing I know his hand has connected with my cheek, the sound cracks through the otherwise silent kitchen. It hurts so much that it burns, the force of his slap sends me flying onto the floor. I grab my cheek with my hands as tears stream down my face. My cheek is hot and throbbing and I just sit on the kitchen floor and cry.

Learn when to shut up for god sake.

Kevin turns and storms up the stairs.

I quickly pull myself together, grab my little bag from last night, shove my phone, bank card and keys in it and head for the front door.

CHAPTER FOURTEEN

O nce I am outside I quickly get in my car, start the engine and start driving. I have absolutely no idea where I am going I just know I can't be here. I drive for a few minutes and then pull over on the side of the road. I need to go somewhere, I can't just drive around aimlessly all day. I get out my phone and call Celine. Voicemail. After trying twice more I give up. She is with Danny and is probably laid up in bed with him still. I can't go to my Mum and Dads looking like this, Ami can't see me in this state. I literally have nobody else. I have been totally cut off from everyone I was ever friends with. Without even thinking I open up Facebook, go into my messages, and find Tad's message to me. My thumb hovers over the little phone icon and I bite my lip.

You should stay away from him. All that will come from you meeting up with him is trouble and heartache.

Again I find myself completely ignoring that little sensible voice in my head and calling him.

"Rachel! I'm so glad you called me." He answers almost immediately, as if he has been waiting for my call.

"Tad, hi. Um, I'm sorry I called." Oh god my voice starts breaking as it all becomes too much for me. "I just needed to talk to someone, and, um, well, I don't really have anyone."

"Rach what has happened? You sound upset?"

"I know I said I didn't want to, but are you around any time soon at all? Just to chat. In a public place?"

"Uh, as it happens I have a few days off work and have come back to my house. I live literally behind the beach I first saw you at, we could meet there if you'd like?"

Rachel Lily Blackford, this is your brain speaking. Do not meet this man. Don't you dare ignore me or I will never offer you any advice ever again...

"I will be there in a minute" I smile.

For God sake...

Tad

The beach is deserted when I get there. The sun has well and truly gone into hiding and it looks as if there is a storm coming. I stand by the shore, watching as the waves crash and settle near my feet.

I can feel her before I hear or see her. I turn around and see her standing about ten feet away from me. The first thing I notice is the purple red mark forming on her cheek.

That bastard hit her.

Then I see her eyes, her beautiful, sad eyes. She has been crying, a lot. Her eyes and nose are red. As I turn, she smiles at me. She starts to walk towards me, her eyes never leaving mine. I move closer to her and see a fire in her eyes. Fuck I want her so much.

My stomach is flipping and I have no idea what to say or do. She stops in front of me, so close that her chest is pressing up against mine and the tips of our fingers brush together. I move my hands forward and she winds her fingers around mine. She looks up at me and opens her mouth as if she is about to say something. The next thing I know she has snatched her hand out of mine and pushed her fingers through my hair. She tip toes so her face is level with my own and pushes my lips to hers. My eyes close as our lips meet and electricity rushes through us both. I wrap my free arm around her and my other hand is still locked in hers. I can feel desperation in her kiss, she is crushing my lips where she is kissing me so hard. Her free hand is gripping my hair, my cock is responding to every touch.

"Tad," She half pulls back to say something, whilst still touching my lips with hers. "I don't know what the fuck I'm doing when I am around you."

She closes her eyes tight as if in pain and pushes her soft tongue through my lips, and starts gently flicking my tongue with hers. This is too much. I want to pick her up, rip her jeans off of her and fuck her senseless. She is pushing herself up against me, and the pressure on my hard cock is almost enough to send me over the edge. I gently start to suck her tongue and she moans, it just spurs me on, so I start to nibble her lips and she thrusts her hips forward. Fuck this, in one swift motion I pick her up and she wraps her legs around me. I can feel the heat from her pussy around my cock and I'm worried it's going to burst through my joggers.

Our kiss slows and she pulls her head back to look at me.

"I really did just need someone to talk to you know." She smiles at me and the rests her head on my shoulder.

"What happened?" I ask her whilst carrying her over to a big rock that we can both sit on.

When we reach the rock, I put her down on it.

She looks at me with those beautiful eyes, they look far greyer than the first time I saw her.

"I got home and he had smashed up our house. Glass and books everywhere, furniture on its side. I thought someone had broken in at first. He started asking if I went back to your room last night. I told him no obviously, and then you messaged me."

Oh shit.

"Rach I" –

"Look it's not your fault he is a psycho, all you did was ask if I was ok!"

"And then he did that?" I gently stroke her cheek and she closes her eyes and slowly nods her head.

Fuck I feel awful. I reach down and hold her hand and then we both sit in silence, just watching the waves crash onto the shore.

She looks over at me.

"Sorry about that kiss." She is blushing.

I turn to look at her.

"I'm not."

I start to feel drops of rain.

"Rach come back to mine for a coffee. It's starting to rain and I don't fancy sitting out here getting soaked." She looks worried and starts biting her lip nervously.

"Why don't we run over to Costa instead?"

"I was jogging when you called, I'm a sweaty mess. Just come back to mine, I will behave, I promise."

She smiles at me.

"I won't lie, it's not you I'm worried about." She runs her tongue absent mindedly along her bottom lip and then grazes her teeth over it. I'm not sure I will be able to keep my promise if she keeps doing that.

"Look you had your mad five minutes, everyone is entitled to that. Let's pinky promise to no more kissing, ok?" I offer her my pinky and smile cheekily at her.

She laughs at me and wraps her pinky around mine.

"No more kissing." She repeats.

I stand and offer her a hand to pull her up and then we start walking towards my house.

Rachel

W e are walking along the seafront and there are a couple of houses just up the road. We stop outside one of them and I look at Tad.

"This is your house?"

"It is."

"I love this house! You can see it from the other little beach down the road. I would go and watch all the work that was going on a few years back, when they put that huge glass wall in. I remember thinking to myself how awkward it would be if you forgot your towel and a bus went past the house or something!"

"It seemed a shame to have such an amazing view right outside my house, that I could only see part of through small windows. And I always make sure there are extra towels in the bathroom. And that I remember when the window cleaner is coming" He winks at me and I get butterflies in my stomach.

I know I shouldn't be here, but I just can't help myself. In another life I am positive that me and Tad would be together, and we would be completely in love, and happy. But this is not another life. This is the life I have chosen and I am married to someone else. And even knowing all of this and knowing how hurt I could get, I still can't keep away from him.

He opens the front door for me and his house is stunning. Real wood floors downstairs and a beautiful plush cream carpet leading up the stairs. He leads me into his front room and it is gorgeous. A huge grey corner sofa is in front of a bay window looking out over the sea. The furniture is all pine, and the floor is covered by a soft grey rug. There is a huge TV on the wall opposite the window, and a beautiful stone fireplace underneath it.

"Your house is amazing."

"Thank you." He smiles at me and I can feel my insides melt.

"Coffee?" He asks.

"Mmmm yes please." I follow him into the kitchen. It is massive. It's got to be as big as the entire lower floor of my house! There is an island in the middle where the sink and food prep area is. A beautiful double gas oven is in the middle of the black units on the far side of the kitchen. The floor is made up of dark grey stone. There is a big American style fridge freezer to the left as you walk in.

"Wow."

"You like it?" He smirks at me.

"I love it! I spend half my life in the kitchen, and I dream about one day having a big space like this."

"Do you like to cook?" He asks as he gets some mugs out of a cupboard.

"I love cooking. Mostly baking to be honest but I could spend all day in a kitchen and not get bored at all."

"We have something in common then. I like to watch people cook and then eat the food they have made."

I smile at him. He seems to be able to make me forget about all the shit in my life and just feel happy.

"How do you take your coffee?"

"Milk and one sugar please."

I watch him as he presses a load of buttons on a very posh looking coffee machine. It starts making a noise, and it starts to drip slowly down into the mug. The smell of the coffee filling the kitchen is amazing.

Once the machine has stopped Tad gets some milk from the fridge and finishes our coffees.

"I'm very aware that I am in my sweaty gym stuff," he says to me "I'm just going to run upstairs and shower. I will be ten minutes. Please make yourself at home."

I take my coffee into the front room and sit on his sofa, it is so soft that I sink right down into it. I put my mug on the table and lean back into the lush cushions. I start to think back on the events of the last couple of days that have ended up in me sitting in another man's house after jumping him at the beach.

I hear the shower turn on upstairs and something in between my legs starts to stir. He is going for a shower. He will be naked, wet and soapy. An image flashes in my brain, and I am on my feet before I even know what I am doing.

CHAPTER FIFTEEN

Tad

I stare at myself in my mirror.

Just wash, get dressed and get downstairs.

My cock is rock hard and desperate for release after that kiss on the beach. Without thinking I let my hand grab my length and stroke it once. I close my eyes tight and a thought crosses my mind. Maybe if I come now I will be able to think less with my cock and more with my brain when it comes to talking to Rachel.

I walk into my shower. The hot water feels amazing on my body. I squeeze some shower gel into my hands and start to rub it all over myself. My hand moves slowly down my stomach and on to my cock. I close my eyes and imagine that Rachel is in here with me and it's her touching me. I groan. I start sliding my soapy hand up and down my shaft, all the while remembering Rachel and our kiss, imagining how good it would be to fuck her. To grab handfuls of her sexy arse while I am pounding into her. I imagine all the soft little noises she would make while I am gently tasting every part of her body.

I am close. I start to pump myself harder, desperately chasing the orgasm that I so wish she was giving me. My legs start to shake so I lean over and hold one arm over my head on the wall for support. I'm going to come. It feels like a tingle, creeping up from every corner of my body, until I am desperate for it to stop, but at the same time to keep going forever. I throw my head back as I feel a warm gush of semen shoot out of me, I keep stroking, slower, gripping tighter, and my cock twitches as the last of my come spurts all over the wall of my shower.

Rachel

I stand outside of Tads bathroom door, utterly hypnotised by what I have just seen. I crept up the stairs in the hope of just maybe seeing a glimpse of him naked. I wanted to know what he looked like under all of his clothes. I had no idea what I would see.

He stood in his shower. His tattooed muscles glistening under the water, and his hand stroking his hard, perfect cock. I knew I needed to leave, I shouldn't have been watching him, he had left the door open a crack and I had the perfect view. I tried to move my feet but it was as if they were glued to the floor. I had never seen anything so erotic in my life. I can feel my sex throbbing in my jeans and I am desperate to be touched. I need to leave because if I stay here a moment longer I am going to jump on him and it will be amazing, and awful, and I will end up getting hurt, and hurting him in the process. I sneak quietly back down the stairs and rummage through the drawers in his kitchen for a pen and some paper.

I can hear movement upstairs so I quickly finish my note and hurry towards the door.

I try to close the door as quietly as possible behind me and I walk away. I can't look back.

A storm is in full force outside. The wind and rain lashes at my face which at least hides the tears streaming from my eyes.

I don't know how it happened, but I have definitely fallen head over heels in love with Thaddeus Turner, and there is no way I will ever be able to have him. I always laughed at Celine when she talked about love at first sight. She always told me the only way to believe it was to experience it. I now completely believe her.

Tad

I sit on the stool in my kitchen and read the note that I found.

"Tad,

I'm so sorry, I shouldn't have come here. I can't control myself around you and I don't want either of us getting hurt.
Please don't contact me again.
I so wish things were different.
Rachel xxx"

My stomach falls. What happened? Why did she run off? Why didn't she just talk to me? I run my fingers through my damp hair.

Maybe this is for the best. Maybe she is right. We might both end up getting hurt if we carry on down this path.

But is she not worth that risk?

I have no idea what to do now though. She is obviously in a really bad place. And she has asked me not to contact her again.

I should respect that.

But you won't.

No, of course I won't. This woman makes me feel things that I have never felt before. I have known her all of two days and yet I feel more for her than for anyone I have ever been with before. I have never really had a girlfriend. Just a few dates here and there. It wasn't until I started earning money that women started to throw themselves at me. It's like they smell the money and want to get their claws in. I was burned once or twice at the beginning but since then I have avoided women all together. But I can't help but feel like I was meant to bump into Rachel. The take away coffee put in the wrong mug, the only free table being next to her. Ending up at a fundraiser, sat at her table that same night.

Everything happens for a reason...

Or I went to a coffee shop at a busy time so the staff were too busy to get my order right and there was only one table left. And then by pure coincidence we end up at the fundraiser together...

I check the time. Its 3pm. definitely an okay time for a drink.

CHAPTER SIXTEEN

Rachel

I drove for half an hour until I found a little retail park. I found a lovely little coffee shop and went in. The smell of coffee usually puts a smile on my face as soon as I smell it, but I don't think anything could lift my spirits today. I order an extra-large latte and take a seat at a table next to the counter. It is quiet in here, one soppy love song ends on the radio and another starts up. I recognise it immediately as *I will always love you.*

I put my head in my hands, for fuck sake. Could any other song in the world play please?

A kind looking older lady brings my coffee over to me.

"Cheer up love, it might never happen." She smiles sweetly as I feel my eyes threaten to well up. I try to smile back at her.

"You're right, it probably won't."

She smiles and walks away.

After my third cup of coffee the lady returns and says that she is closing up in a few minutes. She has bought over a little paper bag.

"Here take this home with you dear. It's my secret recipe chocolate fudge cake. It always helps to make me feel a little better." She has such a kind smile. I need to get out of here before my over active eyes start watering again.

"Thank you so much." I take the cake from her and walk over to my car.

I start the engine and see the clock says 6.29pm. How on earth did it get so late?

I have nowhere else I can go. I am going to have to chance going home. If he is still in a state I will just have to go over to Celine's and hope that she is home.

The traffic is absolutely terrible on the way home. It looks like there are hundreds of cars in front of mine, going at a snail's pace. I am less than a mile from my house. There is a side road coming up to the left so I turn down it and park up. I can walk home and pick up my car in the morning. It's freezing outside and my entire body shivers when I step out of my car, but at least it has stopped raining. I can smell frost in the air. I love the cold, it reminds me of Christmas, by far my favourite time of the year. Kevin tends to be working Christmas day, so Ami and I spend the day with my Mum and Dad. They cook the most amazing meal. Then when we are all stuffed with turkey and Christmas pudding we sit and watch *Love Actually*, *It's a Wonderful Life* and *The Muppets Christmas Carol*.

I'm almost sprinting to try to get home quicker, as much as I love the cold, it isn't so fun when I have forgotten my coat!

I get to a large park that is just behind my house. Usually I would walk through it, but now the reason for the traffic becomes apparent. The park is completely blocked off by police tape, and there are police cars and officers everywhere.

As I walk past I recognize a few people from various parties and work related functions over the years. Kevin's colleague David is also here. That's unusual. He wouldn't come out for something small. Something big must have happened. As I walk past he sees me and starts walking away from who he is talking to and towards me. I am so glad it is so dark out so he can't see my face.

"Rachel!" He half runs over to me. "Rachel, hello."

"Oh hi David. Don't often see you out and about. What on earth has happened?"

"Kevin didn't mention anything?" I shake my head looking concerned.

He shifts on his feet uncomfortably and rubs his chin.

"Between you and I? A body was found in the park in the early hours of this morning." A body?! This is such a lovely area, I think the most shocking thing to ever happen here was when some local kids kept stealing our neighbour's milk. "That was why I interrupted your breakfast in bed this morning."

Breakfast in bed? Huh?

"Breakfast in bed?" I ask confused.

"Yeah, when I stopped by this morning Kevin said you were in bed?"

Why would he say that?

"Oh. Uh, he must have been half asleep or something, I stayed out last night..." David's brow creases, he scratches his head in confusion. "But Jesus, a body?! How did they die? Do you know who it is?"

"Uh, we are still looking into it." I can tell something is bothering him, and I can only guess it has something to do with what I said about Kevin.

"Well I guess I'd better leave you to it. I hope you have some answers soon David."

"Yeah, ok. See you soon Rachel."

I start walking off when David shouts after me.

"Oh, Rachel? Can you tell Kevin to call me please?"

"Of course."

Fuck. A dead body right behind my house.

Won't ever be taking the shortcut through the park again.

It's almost 8pm when I get home. He is definitely in as all of the lights are on. My plan is to stay in the hallway next to the front door and call out to him. If he still seems drunk I will leave. Otherwise I will just go straight upstairs and shut myself in my room.

I stand outside the door and take a deep breath.

I open the door to a strong smell of garlic and onions. As I walk through the door I can hear something sizzling from in the kitchen.

He's cooking...?

The house looks spotless. There is a new coffee table in the front room and all the glass and books have been cleaned up. There is even a new rug to replace the one he ruined the night before last. The lights are dimmed, candles are lit all over the place and there is some sort of slow jazz music playing in the background.

The bastard has someone over. In my fucking house. I see red and throw my bag down. Plan abandoned I storm into the kitchen to find Kevin at the cooker, stirring something in a frying pan.

There are candles and a bunch of roses on the table, a bottle of wine is on the side with two glasses next to it.

I feel sick, I know our marriage isn't normal, and I know that he fucks around. But to do it so brazenly in our home; in our daughters home!

"What the *fuck* is going on?" I shout at him.

He turns around and looks surprised to see me.

"Rachel, I didn't hear you come in."

"No clearly not. Expecting company are you?"

"Uh yeah, you."

He scratches his head, almost nervously.

I'm sorry have I crossed over into some alternate universe where I have a husband who cooks me romantic meals?

He obviously sees the look on my face.

"You look confused. Look, have a glass of wine, sit down and just wait for me to put this in the oven." He starts to pour me a glass of wine "I'll be through in a minute. We need to talk."

I take my wine from him and wander into the front room, absolutely bemused.

I take a sip of my wine and start thinking about what the hell is going on.

Maybe he wants a divorce?

This is just so out of the blue for him and I can't really think of any other plausible reason. Maybe he wants me to sign something to say I won't go after his money. He knows that there is absolutely nothing, least of all a lasagna and some wine that would allow me to give him custody of Ami, so this must be about money?

I hear the oven door slam shut and footsteps walking into the front room.

He sits down in the arm chair opposite me and takes a sip of his drink. It looks like he has orange juice in his wine glass.

"Look Rachel, I uh"–

He looks up at me. He looks different. I feel like something has happened that I have missed.

"Jesus Rach, your face. I'm so sorry." His voice breaks and I see tears start to well in his eyes. What the fuck is going on, is he dying?

He walks over and sits on the sofa facing me. This is so weird, I have no idea what to do.

"I am a complete and total cunt. I know that and today I made a promise to myself that I am going to change."

What. The. Fuck?

"After you left this morning I had a bit of a breakdown. I don't know what has happened to me Rachel. I don't know who I am anymore." He starts crying. Like actual real tears...

Oh God.

"I'm going to quit drinking and I'm going to be the best husband you could ever want."

I just stare at him. I am gob smacked. I have no words.

"Rachel?" I keep staring at him. I open my mouth to say something, but there are zero words right now.

My brain is in overdrive. I have a thousand thoughts whirring around in my head and I can't settle on one long enough for me to actually voice anything.

"Please say something." He pleads with me and grabs my hand.

I shudder at his touch and instinctively pull my hand away.

"Uh Kevin. I uh. I mean, um."

That was just a load of sounds. Say actual real words.

"Look, I know I have a hell of a lot of making up to do. Like a hell of a lot, and I don't expect this to happen overnight, but I want you to be happy again."

"When was I happy Kevin?"

That stops him in his tracks and he looks shocked.

"Well in the beginning, when we were just married and were starting out as a family."

"You mean when you first started wearing me down, controlling me, saying and doing vile things to me?"

His face flashes with something I can't make out, and then falls.

"Is there any way back for us Rachel? I promise I can be a better man."

I want to say no. I want to scream and kick and shout at him. I want to tell him that I have met someone else who has made me realise I have never loved him. I've never even come close to loving him. He has never made me happy and more than anything I wish that he would just leave me and Amelia alone to move on with our lives.

But this all just seems too strange.

Maybe I should just see where this goes. Worst case scenario we actually just start getting along better? I suppose long term if we did start to get along, but nothing romantic came from it, he may at least see that we aren't suited for each other and maybe we could split up amicably?

"I don't know, maybe?" I say after a good few minutes of silence.

He looks up at me and smiles.

"That is all I needed to hear." He beams at me.

Any minute now the real Kevin is going to come barging through the door and is going to start screaming for this imposter to leave.

"More wine babe?"

"Uh yeah, ok then." He seems to have just switched within the space of a few hours. Have I imagined how absolutely awful he has been to me for the last eight or so years?

A timer goes off and Kevin jumps up and walks through to the kitchen. I stay glued to the sofa. I have no idea how to act at the moment.

"Rach, food is ready."

"Ok." I stand up and awkwardly make my way into the kitchen. It feels like I have walked into the wrong house. I sit down at the table and watch as he dishes up the only thing I think he has ever cooked. Lasagna with crispy pancetta bits on the top.

He puts a plate of garlic bead in the middle of the table and a bowl of salad next to it and then puts my plate down in front of me.

"Smells great. Thank you." I don't really remember the last time we had a real civilized conversation, and it all just feels too strange.

"It's not a patch on what you cook, but I wanted to prove to you that I am willing to change. I will be a better man Rachel I promise."

I just smile as I take a bit of garlic bread.

"The flowers are for you Rachel, you like roses don't you?"

"Yeah they are lovely." I lie. I hate roses. Always have. Sunflowers are my absolute favourite flower, even Ami knows that. She grew some for me this year at my parents' house and then when they were ready she brought them all home in secret, they were each in individual pots and she scattered them throughout the house. I smile to myself at the memory.

We start to eat and Kevin is jabbering on about some work he wants to get done around the house. He wants to redecorate and put in a new bathroom.

"I was thinking about extending the kitchen too. I know you have always wanted a big kitchen." My eyes shoot up to his and a cautious smile crosses my face. "And then you can completely re do the interior. Whatever and however you want. What do you think?"

"That sounds good. Thank you."

This can't be real? I had a car accident and died didn't I?

If you were dead you'd be here with Tad not Kevin.

My heart hurts just at the thought of Tad. I'm really going to have to forget about him now aren't I...?

We finish eating and Kevin takes our plates to the sink. He starts rinsing them off.

"So David stopped by this morning. He caught me a bit off guard. I was sort of in the middle of that breakdown I told you about. I may have mentioned that I stayed at the hotel with you last night and we got back early this morning and spent the morning in bed. I don't know why I said it but I don't want him to think that I'm a liar, so I would appreciate if he asks you about it that you just go along with what he says."

Oh, shit.

"Oh, um, it's funny you should say that. I actually bumped into David on the way home." He freezes, mid-way through rinsing a plate. "He did mention something about coming to see you, and me being in bed, but I told him that you must have been half asleep as I stayed at the hotel."

He stays silent, then without warning turns and launches the plate across the room at me.

"What the FUCK were you thinking?"

I freeze.

What the hell is happening?

He turns back to the sink, starts grabbing plates and glasses and throwing them at the window.

I stand up and back slowly out of the kitchen. He has actually lost the plot. I need to get out of here.

"WHERE THE FUCK DO YOU THINK YOU ARE GOING." He is charging towards me like an angry bull at a red cloth.

I turn to run and he grabs me by the hair.

"Someone that I work with, at a senior level tells you something that I, your husband has said, and you stand there and call me a fucking liar? Why would you do that Rachel? WHY?"

He is pulling my head backwards and I can feel the room spinning as I'm struggling to catch my breath. Less than two minutes ago things were great, what the hell is happening?

"I'm sorry, he caught me off guard. I just thought you were confused or drunk! Please let go of me Kevin," I beg "I'll go to David and explain it was a misunderstanding. I will tell him we had a fight and you were confused."

The dead body. David's face. That's what this was. He wanted to butter you up so you would be his alibi.

No. No! A wave of nausea hits me and I think I am about to throw up.

"Kevin, what is going on? Why did you really need me to lie for you? Does it have anything to do with the body found right behind our house?"

"Of course it fucking does you stupid cunt. A dead body is found outside my house and now they are going to think I lied about having an alibi. How is that going to look?" His grip on my hair is so hard I am terrified he is going to pull half of my hair out. I need to find a way to get out of here quickly.

"So that's all this was then, you needed me to lie and be your alibi. You had no interest in actually trying to sort things out between us, you just wanted to make sure I would say I was with you all night?" My scalp is burning where he is pulling so hard.

"Just shut up you dumb fuck. I am trying to think."

I can't believe I let myself even start to think that he had changed! How stupid am I? Nobody changes that much that quickly.

"Why would you even need an alibi, why would anyone think you had anything to do with this?"

"I told you to SHUT UP." He pulls my head so hard that I fall backwards. I scurry away from him and pull myself up. He starts to walk towards me, as soon as he is close enough I kick him with as much force as I can possibly manage right in between his legs. He falls to his knees, clutching his balls and I run. My bag is still in front of the door. I grab it, open the door and bolt out of it without even bothering to close it. I am crying so hard that I can barely breathe. I am running as fast as I can and before I have even thought about where I am going I see my little beach in the distance.

CHAPTER SEVENTEEN

Tad

God Sunday telly is awful. I'm sat on my sofa in nothing but my boxers flicking through hundreds of channels and eventually I settle on an old re run of Red Dwarf that I must have seen at least ten times. I check my phone again. I don't know why. I know she isn't going to message. I close the empty pizza box in front of me and start taking it to the kitchen when I hear banging at the door. Frantic, loud banging.

What the hell?

I open the door and there she is. Her face is wet with tears and she is struggling to breathe like she has been running.

"Fuck Rachel, are you ok? What the hell has happened?"

Before I know what is going on she launches herself at me. Her lips are all over mine and her hands are all over my neck and shoulders. I pull away and hold her arms.

"Rachel, stop. Please tell me what's wrong."

"Everything Tad. I need to forget. Please make me forget." She pleads with me and moves her face closer to mine again.

"Rach, I would feel like I was taking advantage of you. Please come and sit down, I'll make coffee. Let's talk."

She pulls her face back to look up at me.

"I don't need to talk, or to drink coffee. I need you Tad, I need this." She puts her hand in between my legs and closes her eyes as she gently squeezes. "Please Tad" she whispers desperately.

With that I lift her up and she wraps her legs around me. I start to kiss her violently. I push her up against the wall. My cock is almost bursting out of my boxer shorts. She starts to move her hips as she rubs herself against my hard bulge. Her kiss becomes frenzied, she thrusts her tongue inside my mouth and I gently nibble it which makes her moan. She grabs one of my hands and guides me to her breast. As I grab it she stops kissing me, bends her head back and bites her bottom lip. I swear I could come just from watching her face while I am touching her. I start to kiss and nibble her neck. She puts both hands on the back of my head and pushes my face harder into her so I bite harder.

"Oh Tad yes!" She pulls my head back and looks at me "I need you to fuck me Tad." She is practically panting.

"Are you sure?" Part of me is still worried that she is doing this for the wrong reasons and will regret it later. The last thing I want to do is hurt her.

"Yes Tad, fuck me. Please." I do not need telling twice. I sling her over my shoulder and carry her up my stairs. I can't believe I am actually doing this.

We get into my bedroom and I put her down. Without a word, she turns me round and pushes me back onto my bed. She takes a step back and kicks off her shoes, then pulls her shirt off over her head. Her breasts are almost spilling out of her bra. She undoes her jeans and slides them down her legs, all the while not moving her eyes from mine. She has the most beautiful body and if I wasn't so mesmerised by the sight of her in front of me, I would be running my hands all over her curves.

She is stood in just her underwear in front of me, giving herself to me completely and it's so fucking sexy. I stand up and walk over to her. I run my fingers through her hair, and gently pull her head to the side so I can go back to kissing her neck.

"You are the most beautiful woman I've ever seen Rach."

She reaches her hands down onto the band of my boxers, and pulls them slowly down while dropping to her knees. She takes my cock in her hand and gently squeezes the end so a bead of pre come spills out of the head. She looks up at me and keeps eye contact as she leans in and licks the tip. This is so fucking hot. She closes her eyes and moves her head forwards, taking me into her mouth.

"Ah fuck!" This feels so good. She has her hand wrapped around the base of my cock and as much of me in her mouth as she can fit. She starts moving her head back and forth and I am going to come if she keeps this up. I pull out of her mouth and pull her up. I start to kiss her again and wrap my arms around her to reach the clasp of her bra. I ping it off and then pull her bra off of her and step back to admire her breasts. They are perfect. I lower my head and take her nipple in my mouth, I gently suck on it and her breathing becomes heavy. I bite down on it and she cries out in pleasure. I turn her around and push her onto my bed.

"How much do you want me?" I ask her

"More than I want anything." She answers, her voice is shaky.

"Show me?" I ask her as I stroke my cock.

She looks almost nervous for a second, until a mischievous look crosses her face. She moves her hand slowly down her stomach onto her black knickers, she pulls aside the crotch revealing her beautiful pink pussy. She is so wet it is glistening. She opens her legs wider and then inserts a finger into herself. She moans and pulls it out, she then uses that finger to beckon me over to her.

"Come and taste how much I want you."

Oh sweet Jesus. I kneel next to the bed and she pushes her finger into my mouth. She tastes amazing, salty and sweet. I grab her knickers, pull them off and throw them somewhere behind me. I open her legs wide and start to trail kisses up her leg until I get to that beautiful pussy. I gently kiss her clit and she throws her head back. I hungrily start to lick and suck at it until she is grinding her pussy into my face. She is close, I want her to come hard. I take two fingers and push them into her. I start to pump them in and out of her.

"Oh fuck Tad, I'm going to come!"

I quicken my pace and suck slightly harder on her clit.

"Aah, fuck, Tad!" Her hands are pushing my face into her and she lifts her hips off of the bed, her pussy starts to tighten and then I feel her orgasm rippling through her in waves around my fingers. Her legs collapse onto the bed and she stills underneath me. I pull my fingers out of her and stand.

"Come here." I tell her, and she sits up. I put my fingers in her mouth and she closes her eyes as she tastes herself.

I need to feel my cock inside her. Now. I lean over to my bedside table, open the drawer and feel around for a condom. I find one, rip it open and slide it over my cock.

I climb onto my bed and pull her on top of me, so we are sitting with our faces millimeters apart.

She suddenly looks nervous.

"You ok?" I ask.

"It has been a really, *really* long time since I did this, start off gently ok?"

I smile at her and kiss her. She pushes me back and lays down on top of me. The head of my cock is just at her opening.

I slowly move my hips upwards to push myself into her. Fuck she is so tight. I watch her face as I gently push more of myself inside her snug wet pussy, she closes her eyes and her mouth slowly opens.

"Are you ok?" I whisper.

She opens her eyes and smiles at me.

"Fuck yes."

I push her down and she takes all of me inside of her. I stay still for a moment and let her get used to me. She lifts herself up and slowly back down again. The image of her beautiful tits bouncing as she fucks me and the feeling of how tight she is, is almost enough to send me over the edge. I concentrate with everything in me on not coming yet. She closes her eyes and starts to fuck me harder. I put my hands on her hips and as she lifts herself, I pull her down hard on my cock.

"Oh god yes." She cries out.

In one swift move I turn her over so she is on her back. She lifts both of her knees up and she gasps as I slide my full length into her. I lean down and kiss her as I start to pound my hips into her. She grabs my arse and pushes me deeper into her.

"Tad, oh Tad, yes!"

I can feel that familiar feeling creeping all over me and I know I am going to come. I want to stay fucking her all night long, but I want to come with her so badly. I quicken my pace and can feel her pussy start to tighten around me.

"Oh shit I am going to come again."

Her words set me off. I slam hard into her as I feel myself coming. Her nails dig deep into my arse and she screams my name as she comes. I keep thrusting until the last of my come has emptied out. And then I fall on top of her. I can feel her pulsating around me. Our breathing is heavy and ragged and I lay on her chest listening to her heart hammering away.

CHAPTER EIGHTEEN

Rachel

I am laid on Tad's bed in post orgasmic bliss. His cock is still inside of me, his head is on my chest and I am running my fingers through his soft hair trying to steady my breathing and make some sense of what just happened.

When I realised where I was going I was just going to ask to sleep on his sofa. I just needed a safe place to go, somewhere to try to get my head around what had just happened at home and work out what to do next.

But then he opened his door in nothing but a pair of boxers. The memory of seeing him earlier in his shower came flooding back to me and before I even knew what I was doing I was all over him.

He slowly moves his hips and pulls out of me. He sits slightly to pull off the condom, ties a knot in it and throws it across the room into a bin.

He lays back down and starts to gently kiss my chest.

He looks up at me smiling.

"Hey."

"Hey you." I beam at him. "That was..." I struggle to find any words to describe how amazing that was. "Incredible." I settle on.

"You are incredible." He says in between kissing my breasts.

I trace the outline of a skull tattooed on his arm. It is part of an entire sleeve that starts at his wrist with a large skull with its mouth wide open, surrounded by lots of intricate line work. Nearer to his shoulder is another skull that looks like it has started to decay. Considering how morbid it is, it is done so beautifully. The line work over the skull then turns into a beautiful rose that covers the top part of his shoulder, leading onto his smooth chest. Behind the rose are black birds, and in front of it on his chest are stars. Under the stars in a beautiful script is the phrase *"What's meant to be will always find a way"*. In theory it would be one of the most mismatched tattoos you could think of. But there, on his gorgeous body, it looks utterly perfect.

"How are you doing?" He asks while stroking the hair out of my face.

"Ask me again when I have recovered." I grin at him.

He pulls himself towards my face and kisses me. Not the same frenzied kisses as before, but soft, gentle kisses. His lips slowly move over mine and part slightly as his tongue gently brushes over my bottom lip. It sends a tingle through me. I nip his bottom lip back and I can feel his cock start to harden next to my leg. I smile, and he pulls away.

"What?"

I nod my head down in the direction of his growing manhood and laugh.

"Have you not had enough yet?"

"Rach, I don't think I could ever have enough of you."

I love him. I actually love him. How has this happened? I have worn pairs of jeans for longer than I have known this man and already I am in his bed, after having mind blowing sex with him and I am completely in love with him. I feel as if in an instant my life has changed irrevocably.

Tad sits up and holds my hands in his.

"I'm just going downstairs to get a drink, can I get you anything?"

"A glass of water would be really nice actually."

"Coming right up."

He grabs his boxers and to my disappointment puts them back on before walking downstairs.

I take a deep breath. I am absolutely spent. For the first time in a long time I feel happy, and calm. I know my life is a total shit storm outside of this room, but I have no reason to think about that now. That is tomorrow's problem.

Tad

I am stood in my kitchen grinning from ear to ear. I have absolutely no idea what happened tonight to her, I really need to ask why she was in such a state when she got here. But even if she hadn't practically begged me to sleep with her, it was clear to see from the look on her face that she wasn't going to take no for an answer.

That was without a doubt some of the hottest sex I have ever had in my life. I have never felt that connected to someone I was fucking before. Normally it's just been about relieving some tension, but this was different. I needed to be inside of her, needed to feel her around me. It was like a piece of me had been missing all my life and I hadn't noticed, but there, buried deep inside of her, I felt complete, like I was exactly where I was supposed to be.

I can hear a buzzing sound faintly coming from my hallway. I wander over and see a bag on the floor. Rachel must have dropped it when she came in and threw herself at me. I smile at the memory. The bag starts to buzz again and I realise she must have a phone in there. I grab the bag and take it up to her.

As I walk into my bedroom I see her on my bed, still naked, fast asleep. Her breathing soft and slow. I can't bear to wake her when she looks so peaceful so I lift my blanket from the end of my bed and cover her over.

The bag starts to buzz again. Three calls in the space of a minute? It might be an emergency. I open the bag and check the phone. Thirty six missed calls and fifty two text messages? What the hell?

I sit down on the bed next to her.

"Rach?" I gently stroke her face to try to gently wake her. "Rachel?"

She sighs and turns her head to the other side.

I look at the phone again and see that all the missed calls and messages seem to be from Kevin. A surge of anger rises up from deep in my stomach. That evil man has abused this amazing woman for most of the last decade. He has used his own daughter as a weapon and terrified Rachel into staying with him. He calls again.

Don't do it. Just put the phone back downstairs and let him sweat.

I look over at Rachel and completely ignore all common sense. I take the phone out of the room and close the door behind me. I answer the call and just listen.

"Rachel? Rachel! Where the fuck are you?"

I stay quiet.

"I swear to fucking god Rachel if you have talked to anyone, ANYONE then I will fucking kill you. Don't for a second think I won't do it. Because of you and your big fucking mouth chances are I've lost everything anyway so I will not think twice about ending you."

I feel the fury bubble over.

"You will not lay a finger on Rachel ever again, do you understand me? And it would definitely be in your best interests to not contact her again."

"Who the fuck is this? Where is my fucking wife?"

"She's asleep in my bed. And she won't be your wife for much longer."

"I swear if it's the last thing I do I will kill you both"–

I hang up on him mid-sentence and turn off her phone.

You should not have done that.

Fuck. I really shouldn't have done that.

But I am not letting her ever go back to that man and I will make sure that she and her daughter are safe and looked after.

I walk back into my room, put her phone back into her bag and leave it on the bedside table.

She looks breathtakingly beautiful, just laying there. I walk around to the other side of the bed and get in, I turn to face her and lift my arm around her to pull her close to me.

This is by far the happiest I have been in a long, long time. It is quite possibly the happiest I have ever been.

Let's just ignore the fact that she is married to someone else who just so happens to be a complete psycho hey?

Yes, let's just ignore that for now.

CHAPTER NINETEEN

Rachel

I open my eyes and am confused for a moment. Then I remember where I am, and whose arms are wrapped around me. The sun is peeking through a gap in the curtains.

I look around Tads room. The wall behind the bed is a beautiful black and grey striped wallpaper. The rest of the walls are a light grey colour. There is a black arm chair in the corner of the room and a big built in wardrobe next to it. I look over to Tad sleeping next to me. Behind him is the huge glass window that covers the front top half of his house. I can see waves crashing on some rocks through the crack in the curtains. The view must be amazing with the curtains open.

As I am looking around I see my bag on the bedside table. I pull my phone out of my bag to check for any messages, and see it's turned off. The battery must have died. I remember seeing a charger in the front room the first time I was here. I put on my shirt and sneak out of the room so I don't wake Tad.

When my phone comes on it is already at 22% battery. I wonder why it turned off?

Once I have unlocked the screen I can see that I have 36 missed calls and 78 new text messages. My stomach starts doing somersaults. I know they are all going to be from Kevin. I open the call log, yep. All the calls are from Kevin. I check my messages. 76 new messages from Kevin, one from voicemail telling me I have twelve new voice messages and one from my dad asking me to call him when I get the chance.

Oh God, I hope Kevin didn't start harassing my parents last night. I ignore the voicemails and texts and call my dad straight away.

"Is everything ok Rachel?" He sounds really worried.

"Yes dad everything is fine, why?" I hate lying to my dad but what can I say?

Actually Dad I think that Kevin is involved in someone's death so I came and shagged the good looking stranger I met two days ago...

"Kevin phoned last night, he was not in a good way. He said that you two had argued and then you stormed out and he wasn't able to get in touch with you." Why would Kevin involve my parents in this for god sake? "Then he said that eventually someone answered your phone but it was a man, who said that you and he were a thing and had been for a while?"

My heart and stomach both drop in unison. Tad answered my phone. To Kevin. And told him we were having an affair? Tears sting at my eyes. Why would he do that? He knows exactly what Kevin is like.

Oh God, what if Kevin takes Ami? My hurt turns to anger. How dare he answer my phone and lie just to get one over on Kevin.

"Rach?"

"Dad, uh, I think Kevin is in some trouble at work. We had a huge fight about it last night and I stormed out and went to a friends. Everything else is just a figment of Kevin's very vivid imagination."

I need to make sure that Ami is kept away from Kevin at all costs until I have done a serious amount of damage control. Plus I need to speak to the police to find out exactly what he is hiding with this dead person.

"Listen Dad, I can't say too much right now, mainly because I don't know exactly what is going on, but if Kevin calls you again, don't answer. Don't tell him where you are. And if you can, try to get Ami's phone away from her"-

"What"-

"Dad I know, please just trust me on this." I take a deep breath. I need to be honest with him, to make sure Ami is kept safe. "I'm not even sure what has happened, but he has lost it Dad. Like seriously lost it. I'm going down to the police station to speak to someone today about him. But it is absolutely vital that Kevin has no contact with Ami until I have worked out what is going on."

"I'm not happy about being kept in the dark here Rachel."

"It's not on purpose Dad, I'm pretty in the dark myself. Just give me until this evening. I will call you back and tell you everything I can."

"Okay princess. You are safe aren't you?"

I have absolutely no idea.

"Of course I am." I lie. "Tell Ami I love her loads and will speak to her this evening."

"I love you Rachel."

"Love you too Daddy."

I hang up and see Tad in the doorway out the corner of my eye.

How dare he stand there, half naked and gorgeous, when he has betrayed me like he has. And how dare my own stupid body betray me by being so turned on by him right now.

I opened up to this man, opened up to him more than I have ever opened up to anyone. And he doesn't care. He doesn't care about what happens to me once I leave here. Maybe he gets his thrills sleeping with married women and then taunting their husband's about it.

"Good morning beautiful." He walks over to me, sits down on the sofa and leans in for a kiss. I turn my head away from him. He pulls back.

"What's wrong?"

I can't even look at him.

"How dare you." I meant for that to come out angry and defiant, instead it ended up coming out as barely a whisper.

"Rach?"

He touches the top of my arm. I close my eyes to try to hold back the tears and shrug his hand off of me.

"Rachel, please, talk to me?"

I keep staring out of the window. I am so hurt right now, I feel broken. I trusted this man. I know I barely know him, but for whatever crazy reason I trusted him, and like a total idiot I managed to fall in love with him! Maybe this isn't love at all. Maybe this is just lust and I have no idea because I've never had the opportunity to experience it before.

If it's not love then why the hell does this hurt so badly?

I feel him get up. He walks in front of me and crouches down so he is looking at my face. Silent tears escape my eyes as I open them.

"Why did you do it?" I whisper. It hurts to speak. It hurts to breathe. In nine long years Kevin never managed to hurt me like Tad has now.

His face falls as he realises I know.

"Rachel, I"–

"I don't even want to hear it. I trusted you. God only knows why, but I did. I told you things I have never told anyone. Of all people, you know what he is like. You saw him the other night! And now you have told him we have been having an affair." My tears are replaced by anger. "Why?"

"Rachel, I swear I never said we had been having an affair!"

"It doesn't matter if you did or didn't! You answered my phone, my personal phone. A man answering my phone late at night is enough for anyone to think we had been sleeping together!"

"I know I shouldn't have answered it. I am so sorry. I don't even know why I did it. I just saw his name flash on the screen and I got so angry with him for the way he has treated you. The things he has done to you."

"So you thought it would be a brilliant idea to tell him we had just fucked?" I shout loudly at him.

Tad looks shocked.

"Rachel I didn't say anything like that."

"What did you say then?"

"He was going on about how if you had talked to anyone he was going to kill you. I lost it. I told him that he wouldn't ever lay a finger on you and to leave you alone. And" –

He closes his eyes and looks down at the floor.

"And what?" I can feel my anger bubbling up. I am going to explode in a minute. This is too much for one person to deal with in such a short space of time.

"And he asked where his wife was. So I told him. You were asleep. In my bed. And that you wouldn't be his wife for much longer. I'm sorry Rach."

"Don't. Just DON'T." I scream at him as I jump up off the sofa. I storm off upstairs to get my clothes. I need to get out of here. He follows me silently. I wish I had put my underwear back on this morning as from where he is walking he has a perfect view of my backside.

I grab my jeans from the floor and start to look around for my bra.

"Rachel, I am so sorry. I knew it was wrong. I knew I shouldn't answer your phone. But I knew that I could never let you go back to him."

"I don't want to hear it Tad."

"Please, I am begging you, hear me out. I can't let you walk out like this. I can't run the risk you won't ever see me again."

"It's not a risk, it's a fact. You clearly don't care about me at all or you wouldn't have put me and my daughter in this fucking position."

"It's because of how much I care about you Rachel. I know it's crazy. I know we have only just met, but, fuck! I feel like you're the part of me that has always been missing without me even knowing I was missing it in the first place. I can't let you go back to that monster. I won't. I will protect you and Ami from him, I swear it."

"Don't you dare say my daughter's name!"

I turn to look at him. I fucking hate my body right now. I am so angry with him, I am so hurt, yet seeing him standing in front of me in just his boxers is making me extremely aware that I have nothing on my bottom half.

I see my bra over by the arm chair and go to pick it up. He follows me over like a little lost fucking dog.

"Please leave me alone Tad. I need to get out of here and attempt to make some sense of the steaming heap of shit that is my life right now."

I grab my bra, and turn around to go to the bathroom. Tad is standing in front of me and without warning he drops to his knees.

"Rachel, I am begging you. I have never fucking begged for anything in my life before. Please, please don't leave like this."

Without thinking I grab his head, and pull his face in between my legs. I have no idea what I am doing. I need to get out of here, but part of me feels like I need him more.

He doesn't need any persuasion and immediately pushes his tongue through my soft folds. His hands grab my hips and he pulls me closer so his greedy tongue can reach further. He starts flicking it frantically over my clit.

He is so fucking good at that. My breathing quickens. I know I need to get out of here and I don't know what I hoped to achieve by pushing his face into me, but now I can't move. He removes a hand from my hip, and moves it to the opening of my sex. He pushes two fingers deep inside of me with such force that it makes me cry out. He starts frantically fucking me with his fingers and licking and sucking me until my knees feel like they are about to give way. I am grabbing fistfuls of hair and pushing my hips rhythmically along with his fingers. My insides start to pulse and I feel a fire growing in the pit of my stomach. I explode around his fingers and feel a warmth spread out to every corner of my body.

He pulls his fingers out of me and stands, looking at my face.

I want to feel his cock inside me, I want him to come inside of me and I want to feel every single part of it.

I want to completely own this man. Even though it will probably be the last time I ever see him.

I turn my back on him and bend over the chair. He starts to walk away.

"Where are you going?" I stutter.

"Condom."

"Do we really need one?"

His eyes sparkle.

"I know I don't..." He replies.

"Then fuck me Tad."

I turn back around as he quickly pulls his hard cock out while walking towards me. He enters me in one swift thrust. He fills me up to the point it hurts. But it is the very best kind of pain. He slowly pulls back and then slams hard into me again.

"Ah fuck!"

He starts pounding into me, like he knows. He knows that this is it for us. He has broken my trust and this is the last time I will see him.

I can hear him hissing, he must be getting close.

"Harder." I whimper. "Harder, please!"

He grabs hold of my hips and pulls me toward him with every powerful thrust.

"Yes... yes... oh fuck yes!"

I reach out and grab onto the back of the chair, I'm gripping on so tight that my knuckles are turning white and I am starting to lose the feeling in my fingertips.

This feeling is like nothing I've ever felt. I'm there, I'm right there. It's like I have jumped from a plane, but instead of falling, I am floating in mid-air, floating in a constant state of pleasure, excitement, exhilaration. It feels so good I don't want it to ever end, but I do, because I know what comes next is so much better. I feel like I am just waiting for one final tiny movement to knock me out of the air. My sex is clenching fiercely around his rock hard cock and with one more perfect thrust I feel my whole body start to shudder, starting in between my legs and rippling out to every single part of my body. He keeps plunging hard into me until my legs slump and I fall forwards into the chair.

He hasn't come yet. He is prolonging this is much as he possibly can. He doesn't want it to end, and neither do I. But I can't get hurt by anyone else.

He lifts me up and carries me over to the bed. He throws me down on my back, lifts my legs over his shoulders and leans over me. He is sliding his erection over my soft folds, teasing me. I am struggling to catch my breath. The orgasms Tad gives me are like drugs. I just can't seem to get enough. I grab his tight arse and pull him into me. He lets out a low groan and closes his eyes. He slowly starts to push in and out of me. I look down and watch his perfect cock sliding in and completely filling me up, stretching me to fit his whole length. I can feel every part of him and it's amazing.

He is slowly fucking me, taking his time, savouring every moment of me. It's too intense.

I meet his thrusts with my own, I slam back into him, and he screws up his eyes tight and throws his head back.

"Yes, harder!"

He looks back down and slams into me, he quickens his pace and fucks me so hard I feel like I might rip in two.

I throw my arms behind me and grab the blanket to try to hold on for dear life as I feel my orgasm brewing. I turn my face into my arm, and feel his hand grasp my chin and pull my face back so I am looking at him.

"I want to see your face when I make you come." He growls at me.

All of a sudden the earth stops and I melt into the bed, my hips are jerking and my sex is clamping so hard around Tad.

"Oh God Rachel! I'm coming!"

He fucks me even harder as I feel him emptying himself into me. The sensation of his come filling me up is too much and sets off another orgasm almost immediately after my last. I close my eyes and start to see stars.

He slumps down on my chest and I feel his cock twitch inside of me as I pulse around him. I kiss him gently on the cheek, he rolls off of me and lays on the bed while he catches his breath. If I don't leave now I will never be able to.

I stand up grab my clothes and walk into the bathroom without a word said from either of us.

Tad

I sit up and watch her walk away.

What was that?

One minute she is leaving, and then the next she is pushing my face into her gorgeous pussy.

I thought for a minute she had forgiven me for being such a fucking idiot, but the way she was fucking me just seemed different to last night. The first time it felt desperate, but desperate like she needed to have me, it didn't matter the consequences, she wanted me more than anything. This time it felt desperate in a whole different way, like she was desperate to feel me one last time.

I can't lose her.

I've never felt this way about anyone before.

I'm falling in love with her.

I pull some boxers on and go to the bathroom door. I have no idea what I can say to her, I know I was an idiot, but it came from a good place. I just want to protect her. He was threatening to kill her! I flipped!

I hear the lock slide open and my stomach lurches. She opens the door, looks straight past me and walks out. I turn to follow her silently.

She walks into my front room and grabs her bag from the table.

"Rachel, please don't go."

She walks up to me and gives me a kiss on the cheek.

"Goodbye Thaddeus."

I crumple to the floor as the door slams shut behind her.

I think she was the one. And I fucked it up so badly I am never going to see her again.

CHAPTER TWENTY

Rachel

After leaving Tad, I realised I had nowhere to go. I couldn't risk going home, so I walked to my car and drove straight to Celine's.

I look an absolute mess. I have a hand shaped bruise across my throat, my cheek is purple, and my eyes are completely red and swollen from the insane amount of crying I have done over the last couple of days.

I ring the doorbell and prepare myself.

She opens the door, and her face falls as soon as she looks at me.

"Hi." I almost whisper.

"You turn up at my house looking like that and the first word out of your mouth is Hi? Jesus babe, come here."

She pulls me in for a hug and everything comes spilling out of me at once. Kevin assaulting me at the fundraiser, realising he was trying to use me as an alibi, the reasons behind why he needed an alibi. And Tad. He has broken my heart. Celine pulls me through her front door and we sink to the floor as I'm sobbing into her chest. I hear footsteps coming down the stairs that stop abruptly.

"Dan put the kettle on babe then make yourself scarce for a bit please."

"Yeah. Ok, no problem. Is she ok?"

I feel her shrug.

"I'm so sorry Cel." I sob into her.

"Hey don't you apologise. Let it all out babe, then tell me what the hell has happened so I can stop worrying, or worry more, we will see.

I tell her everything. *Everything.*

Two cups of coffee later and I am getting to the part where I ended up fucking Tad last night.

"Let me just stop you for two minutes." She interrupts. "I need to make sure I am getting this. So this guy, Thaddeus, stops Kevin from attacking you, you then have a drink with him and share all your deepest darkest secrets. Kevin then smacks you across the face because he thinks you slept with Thaddeus"-

"Just call him Tad."

"Okay, Tad... so you meet up with Tad and snog his face off on a beach? Am I right so far?"

"Yes. But in my defence I did call you first but you were too busy having amazing sex!"

"So after you snog, you go back to his house and do the perviest thing in the world and watch him get himself off, then you leave without so much as a thank you?"

I put my head in my hands.

"You are making it sound worse than it was!"

"You get home to find Kevin has had a brain transplant, but then it turns out he was just trying to sweet talk you into giving him an alibi because he has murdered someone?"

"I didn't say he murdered anyone, but he obviously has something to do with it. I need more coffee for the rest of this story."

"There's more?!" Her eyebrows shoot up in surprise.

We walk into the kitchen and I flick the switch on her kettle.

"Have you spoken to the police yet?"

"Um, no. I meant to last night but I got a bit side tracked..."

"Side tracked...?"

I start pouring water into our cups.

"I had sex with Tad."

There is silence for a long time, I look over my shoulder to see her standing with her mouth wide open.

"What?! How?! I mean- You have known the guy two minutes!"

"It gets worse..."

"How is that possible?!" Her eyes look like are about to pop out of their sockets.

"So I genuinely only went round for somewhere to sleep and so I could phone the police. But I turned up and he opened the door in nothing but underwear... so I sort of threw myself at him and begged him to have sex with me." She opens her mouth as if to speak so I hold my hand up to her face.

"Hang on, I'm not there yet. After we had sex, I passed out on his bed and he took it upon himself to answer my phone when Kevin called, and he told him we had just slept together." Her mouth drops open once again.

"Even though you told him what Kev said he would do to you if you tried to leave him?"

I nod.

"I found out this morning, and had it out with him. Then we had sex again and I left without a word. And that's it."

She stays silent for a moment while trying to process everything.

"You should have warned me, this needed vodka not coffee."

"Oh, sorry I forgot, just one more thing. I now believe in your stupid love at first sight bullshit, because as it turns out, I'm in love with him. I am pretty sure he is my soulmate. But now he has gone and fucked it up so spectacularly I will never be able to forgive him or trust him again."

She walks over to her freezer and pulls out a bottle of vodka. Before even closing the freezer door she has taken a swig out of the bottle.

I can't help but giggle. This is why she is my best friend.

A couple of hours later I am feeling better. Celine ran me a bath and Danny went out to get us all McDonalds. After both of us getting through half a bottle of vodka at 11am, the grease was definitely needed!

I'm sat on the sofa when my phone rings. *Unknown number.*

Me and Celine look at each other.

"Answer on speaker." She says.

"Hello?"

"Oh hello is this Rachel Blackford?"

"Yes it is, who is speaking please?"

"My name is DC Robins. I need to speak to your husband as a matter of some urgency, but I've been unable to get in touch with him. Would you happen to know where he is?"

"Can I ask what this is regarding? Is this a work thing or is he in some sort of trouble?"

"I'm afraid I can't really discuss that with you at this time. But do you know where he is?"

"No, I'm sorry. I haven't seen him since about 8pm last night." I pause and decide to just ask outright. "Um, does this have anything to do with the dead body that was found last night?"

"Like I said I can't really discuss that with you right now. Is there any chance you would be able to pop into the station? Just so I can ask you a few things?"

"Um, I suppose so. Should I be worried?"

"No no. I just have a couple of things I need to speak with you about. I am at the station now and will be here for most of the afternoon, if you could pop by shortly. I know you don't live too far away."

"No problem. See you soon."

"Thank you Mrs. Blackford."

Celine looks at me.

"I'm coming with you. I'll get Danny to drive."

My heart swells at the love I have for this woman. She has never once let me down. She is like the sister I never had.

CHAPTER TWENTY ONE

Celine and I walk up to the reception at the police station.

"Hi, I'm here to see DC Robins." God I hope I don't bump into anyone I know here looking the way I do. I wanted to put some make up on to try to cover all the bruising, but Cel convinced me that it's about time I let people know what Kevin is really like.

The receptionist asks for my name and makes a call.

"If you go down that corridor and turn left, you will see his office on the right hand side."

"Thank you."

Celine grabs my hand as we walk to his office.

DC Robins.

I knock.

"Come in".

I open the door to find a guy in his late forties with big square glasses and grey hair sitting at a desk that is piled high with papers next to his two computer screens.

He takes off his glasses and stands as we walk in.

"Mrs. Blackford lovely to meet you." He holds out his hand. I shake it.

"Please call me Rachel. This is my friend Celine."

She shakes his hand and he points to the chairs in front of his desk.

"Rachel, thank you for coming in so quickly. I don't suppose you have managed to get in touch with your husband have you?"

"Um no, sorry I didn't try. We aren't really speaking at the moment. I look down at my hands and start fidgeting with them absent mindedly.

"Would it be possible for us to speak in private?"

"No its ok, Celine is my best friend. I need her here." She grabs hold of one of my hands on my lap and smiles at me.

"Very well." He smiles at us both, looks at my face and his smile turns to concern. "May I ask what happened to your face?"

Oh God, this is it. There is no going back from here. It is time to stick to my guns and get away from Kevin. If anything, the last few days with Tad have shown me that there is the possibility of real happiness away from my toxic marriage.

"Um, me and Kevin had a falling out."

"A falling out that resulted in him hitting you."

I look down at my lap and nod. DC Robins is writing down notes as I am talking.

"Can I ask what the falling out was about?"

"Well the most recent one was because I had told someone that Kevin works with that I didn't spend Friday night with him. I bumped into David Thompson on the way home as there were police everywhere by my house. He said he stopped by that morning and Kevin said I was in bed. I explained that Kevin must have still been half asleep as I stayed out that night and Kevin went home alone."

"Hmm." He is writing furiously.

He opens a file and pulls out a photo. He puts it in front of me. It's a photo of a young woman. Early twenties, blonde, very pretty.

"Do you know who this is?"

I'm confused.

"No. Sorry, should I?"

He looks nervously at Celine, and I nod for him to continue.

"This is Sally Barker. It was her body that was found yesterday." That is awful, she is so young, but why would I know her?

"I'm so sorry that you are having to hear this from me Rachel, but she and your husband had been having an affair for about six months."

I'm numb. I suddenly feel like I am looking at myself, like I am watching one of those crime dramas on TV. None of this feels real. I take a deep breath and try to ignore the sick feeling in my stomach.

"And you need to speak to Kevin because you think he killed her?" The words are falling out of my mouth, I have no control over them. I don't feel like I am actually here anymore.

"We just need to run through some things with him. As you have told us, his alibi was being at a hotel in London with you. However, after speaking to you, David called me to let me know that you weren't with Kevin at all that night, and sure enough we checked CCTV from the Four Seasons that shows him being escorted out and put in a cab. We called the cab company who said that on the way to your house, Kevin asked to stop somewhere first. He picked up Miss Barker and they went back to your house."

I can feel he contents of my stomach rising into my throat. He had been sleeping with someone else in my house. Oh God.

He killed her in my house.

The room starts to spin.

"Rach, you ok?" I feel Celine's arm wrapped around my shoulders.

"No." I whisper. "Can you get me some water or something please?"

"You sure you'll be ok with me gone."

I nod. When I hear the door close behind me I look at Robins.

"Please don't sugar coat this; He killed her didn't he?"

He lets out a long sigh.

"I'm going to be honest with you Rachel, it does look that way. But we really need to speak to him. This could all just be a misunderstanding." Something in his eyes tells me that he doesn't believe that for a second. "Please, if you hear from him at all, let me know immediately." He hands me a card with all of his details on.

I nod.

"Unless there is anything else you can think of that might be important you can leave, I can imagine how hard this all must be for you. I would advise against staying at your house for the time being. Do you have somewhere you can stay?"

Again I just nod.

I stand up and leave.

I close the door behind me and have to steady myself against the wall. The floor feels like it is moving under my feet. A searing pain shoots through my chest and I struggle to catch my breath. Darkness starts to creep into my vision from every corner.

"Rachel? Rachel!"

Through the slit of light in between the black I see Celine running towards me. And then nothing.

CHAPTER TWENTY TWO

Tad

At some point in the day I manage to drag myself from the floor of my hallway on to my sofa. A bottle of alcohol has miraculously appeared in my hand. I don't even know what it is. All I know is the burn on the back of my throat as it goes down is extremely welcome.

I can't believe I have been so stupid.

I stare at her beautiful photo. Her hair is blowing in a breeze and she looks like she is laughing. A wayward strand of hair flies over her face, and I imagine tucking it behind her ear and kissing her soft cheek.

I have had two missed calls from Scott, three from Suze and a voicemail from her. I can't bring myself to listen to it and I don't want to speak to anyone.

I have no idea how long I've been sitting here. It could be minutes or hours, I have no clue.

I feel my phone start to vibrate next to me and I almost fall off my sofa when I see it's a Facebook call, from Rachel. My heart starts beating so hard it feels like it might burst through my chest.

"Fuck, Rachel, I am so pleased you called me"–

"This isn't Rachel." A woman's voice that I don't recognize interrupts me. My breathing stops.

*Why is she calling me from Rachel's phone?"

"I'm Celine, Rachel's best friend," she continues. I remember Rachel telling me about her the other night. "Listen, I am at the hospital with Rachel. She is pretty out of it but she keeps saying your name. I'm not sure but I think she wants to see you." My stomach drops, in hospital why?

"What happened, why is she is hospital, is she ok?!" I stand and frantically run my hands through my hair.

"I'm not sure, she lost consciousness and we had to call an ambulance. The doctors are worried she might have had a heart attack."

The words hit me in the gut like a ton of bricks, I can't hear a word Celine says next as my brain shuts down.

A heart attack was what killed Seb. Just a few weeks ago. I have to get to her. I have to make her better. I cannot lose her.

"Which hospital and where?"

After what seems like an age waiting for a cab I am running through the corridor of A&E. I sprint to the reception.

"Um I am looking for Rachel Blackford, can you tell me where she is?"

"Are you family?"

"Yes I am her fiancé."

I had to lie or I wouldn't have been able to see her. The woman starts typing on her computer. Why is it taking so long?

"Please, she was bought in by ambulance a short while ago, suspected heart attack." As I say the words, tears threaten my eyes.

This can't be happening again.

"If you go through those double doors and down the corridor you will reach another set of doors with a buzzer, ring the bell and someone will let you in." She offers me a sympathetic smile. I shout my thanks at her as I run off in the direction she is pointing in.

I buzz and wait. A sign above the intercom reads *"We get very busy and are sometimes unable to answer immediately. Please only ring once and someone will let you in as soon as possible. Thank you."*

Fuck that.

I buzz again.

In reality I have probably been waiting less than a minute, but it feels like the single longest minute of my entire life. Finally someone answers.

"Can I help?"

"My fiancée, Rachel Blackford. I need to see her."

The door makes a clicking sound and I yank it open with such force it slams into the wall behind it.

I walk into a large room with about ten curtained off bays. It's so loud in here with different voices and machines bleeping. There are Doctors and nurses rushing about all over the place.

Please let her be ok.

I suddenly don't want to find her. I don't want to know. What if... God I can't even think it.

A nurse walks up to me.

"Are you here for Rachel Blackford?"

"Y-yes, I am. Is she ok?" She starts walking to the far side of the room and I follow her.

"She is still out of it from the medication we have given her, but she is stable. The Doctor will be in shortly to discuss the results of her tests."

We get to the last bay and she pulls the curtain back for me.

I am suddenly terrified. Seb was stable. He was ok. He woke up and we laughed and joked. We planned a trip to Vegas. And then in the blink of an eye he was gone.

A woman walks over to me from the other side of the curtain. She is almost as tall as me, dark honey skin and black hair set into tight curls. She has one of those faces that just look extremely kind. Her eyes are red and her makeup has smudged around her face from where she has obviously been crying.

"Hi." She says with a smile. "I'm Celine, you must be Tad?"

"Yes. Hi. How is she?"

I look over at the bed and see Rachel laying on the bed. She looks peaceful. She isn't wearing a shirt, and has about fifteen wires coming out from underneath the white sheet that is covering her chest.

"She is ok. She had me really fucking worried for a moment. She just went down clutching her chest and then I couldn't wake her up. It's ok though, they now don't think it was a heart attack. Her blood pressure was sky high when we were in the ambulance and even with medication it was taking a while to go down. But it has stabilised now. Just waiting for a doctor to come round to speak to us."

It wasn't a heart attack. I feel like I could cry I am so relieved.

I walk over to the bed and sit on the chair next to her, Celine walks over to the other side and is nervously biting her nails.

"So she asked for me?"

"In the ambulance I was trying to ask her if she wanted me to call her parents but she just kept saying no and to call you. We had talked earlier today and I know she was pretty upset with you so I ignored her for a bit, but then when we got here she kept asking where you were. So I thought I had better call you."

Oh shit. Rach told her about what I did.

I just nod, then grab Rachel's hand with both of mine and stroke my thumb over her fingers.

There is a slightly awkward silence hanging in the air.

"Celine?" She looks up at me. "What happened last night, before Rachel came to mine?"

"She didn't tell you?" She looks shocked. I shake my head and she smirks to herself.

"So she did literally just jump on you the second you opened the door!" She laughs. "I thought she was just giving me the cliff notes version!" I half smile and can see why she and Rachel are so close.

She starts to bite her nails again.

"I'm not really sure I should say what happened. It's not really any of my business."

"Please, I'm worried. When I decided to be the world's biggest dick and answered her phone, that arsehole said that he would kill her if she talked to anyone. What is he so worried about her saying?"

Her eyes widen and she looks horrified.

"He said what?"

"He said that if she had talked to anyone he would end her, and that because of her big mouth he had lost everything."

She looks totally dismayed.

"Oh fucking hell." It's barely a whisper.

What the hell am I missing here?

"Celine please, your worrying me."

She takes a deep breath and closes her eyes.

"The police think that Kevin killed someone."

Oh my fucking God.

"He tried to make Rachel lie and give him an alibi, but she had already bumped into someone and mentioned she spent Friday night at the hotel alone. He completely flipped out and went psycho on her, and then she ran to your house."

This is a hell of a lot to process. No wonder she is laying here now, unconscious and blue lighted in to hospital from high blood pressure.

Her husband is a murderer. And he said he was going to kill her.

Shit, no wonder she reacted the way she did when I answered the phone. I knew he was a total cunt, but I didn't think he was capable or murder.

We sit in silence for a while, and then Rachel starts to stir.

I feel her hand tighten around my own and she starts to open her eyes.

She squints through them as the lights in here are so bright.

"Rachel sweets, you back with us?" Celine is hovering over her. "I'm just going to go and let the nurse know that you're awake babe." She stands up and rushes through the curtain to find someone.

"Where I am?" her voice is deep and croaky.

"You're in hospital. You collapsed."

"Tad? What- Why are you here?" She tries to sit up.

"Woah, stay there until the doctor has been in. Just relax. Celine called me. Apparently you were asking for me."

"I was?" She scrunches up her face in confusion as she tries to remember. "I don't really remember anything. I was at the police station, and then the next thing I know I'm laid down in the back of an ambulance, with sirens going off and people trying to shove needles into me."

"I'm just so pleased you are ok."

She turns to look at me and half smiles.

Celine walks back through the curtains, straight over to the bed, sits on the side and throws herself on to Rachel.

"Don't you ever scare me like that again you hear me?! I've aged fifty years since I got here, I got called fucking ma'am by the guy in the cafeteria. Ma'am for Christ sake!"

They both laugh.

"I'm sorry! What happened?" Rachel asks, obviously confused.

"After you got out of Robins office you went all pale and started clutching at your chest and then you just passed out. I couldn't wake you up at all so I called an ambulance. We thought you'd had a heart attack. Turns out you've just stressed yourself out too much woman. Your blood pressure was ridiculously high."

"So all this is because I have high blood pressure?"

"Probably. The nurse said she will send a doctor in to see you now that you're awake."

If it wasn't for the fact that the two of them looked nothing alike, I'd have thought they were sisters. They must have been friends for years, the way they look at each other its plain to see that they care about each other huge amounts.

I hope Celine doesn't hate me for what I did. If she does then I have no hope of fixing this. But a small part of me, just a tiny part, is optimistic that maybe Rachel will forgive me. And Celine can't hate me too much or she wouldn't have called me.

"Can I get anyone a coffee or something?" I'll give them a bit of time alone and just go for a walk. I need to clear my head too. This morning has been crazy. Never mind this morning, this whole weekend has just been totally insane.

"Oh God a coffee would be amazing." Celine replies with a huge smile on her face. She looks like a different person now that Rachel has woken up.

"And me" – Rachel starts but Celine interrupts.

"Just water for you woman until the doctor has been around!"

Rachel suddenly looks horrified.

"Oh God, caffeine is bad for blood pressure isn't it! I'm going to have to switch to decaf."

Me and Celine burst into laughter at the look on Rachel's face. Of all the things she should be concerned about and caffeine is her main worry!

CHAPTER TWENTY THREE

Rachel

I watch Tad walk out of the curtain and I don't know whether to hug or hit Celine.

"Why did you call him?" I hiss angrily at her.

"Babe, you kept asking for him over and over, you were crying and asking why he wasn't here. I figured even if it was the pain relief they had given you it was obviously coming from somewhere."

"And..?" I question her. There is clearly another reason.

"Well, I know he fucked up. But I kept thinking, you turned up in a state at his house and then fucked him. He probably thought you and Kevin were over and that he was protecting you or something."

"Hmmm."

"Look, I definitely think it says more about how much he cares for you as opposed to how little. Rach, you should have seen the state of him when he came running in here. He was an absolute mess. He lied to the nurses that he was your fiancé."

"He did what?" I smile at the thought.

"Yeah, they mentioned it to me as they thought it was funny that *Mrs.* Blackford's fiancé was here." She smirks.

Celine hands me a cup of water and I take a sip.

Maybe I was a bit hard on him. I mean, yes he did mess up but regardless of who was on the phone, it is my phone. My private property. I have had years of being watched and having my phone searched. I shouldn't have to worry about anyone else doing that. But he was probably so confused. He opens to door to find me stood there, a sobbing mess and then I throw myself at him and offer no explanation for anything. I think I owe him a conversation at the very least.

Just the Tad opens the curtains and walks through with two large coffee cups and a bottle of water.

God that coffee smells so good!

"How are you feeling?" He asks me with a kind smile.

"I'm ok, wish this doctor would hurry up though, I want to go home"-

And then it hits me. I can't go home. Where am I going to go? I can never step foot in that house again knowing what he did in there. Oh God and Ami, what am I going to tell her? She goes on holiday with her Nanny and Gramps, and comes home to Mummy living in a different house and Daddy being locked away for murder.

"Rach...? What's wrong?" Tad looks worried.

"Nothing, I just- Well, everything! I can't ever go back to my house, I have nowhere to live and what do I tell Ami?"

"Right, first off calm down, this is what got you in here in the first place." Celine comes and sits next to me on the bed. "You have me, you can stay with me for a few days, I have a blow up bed I can put in my office that you can sleep on. And for now, you just tell Ami that Daddy is having a bit of trouble with work so she won't be able to see him for a little while."

"You know for a fact that there is no way she will just accept that! She will want to know exactly what problem, where he is, when he will be back. Plus this is murder! And not just any murder, he is the Commissioner of the Police! This is going to be all over the papers!"

"Look stop panicking, we will cross that bridge when we need to. We can phone your parents in a bit and get them to try to keep her away from the news and papers and then once they have questioned him, we will have a better idea of what we need to do."

Celine always knows what to say to calm me down. She knows me so well, knows exactly how I think so she knows how to fix everything. I will have to find somewhere more permanent to stay though. Her office is tiny, I'm not even sure an air bed would fit! I have a key to Mum and Dad's and I know they will be fine with me staying there, so I will do that until I can work something out. It's not even like I have any money as everything is in Kevin's name, so I have no idea how I am going to do anything.

"Thanks babe, I'm just going to stay at Mum's for a little while. God I can't believe I don't even have any access to any accounts. I'll have to sell some bits or get a loan out or something. What a bloody mess."

Tad looks like he is about to say something when a man comes through the curtains. He is wearing green scrubs and has a stethoscope around his shoulders.

"Mrs. Blackford? Hi I'm Doctor Patterson." He walks towards me with a hand outstretched. He is in his late forties, grey hair and very prominent frown lines. "How are you feeling now?"

"Not too bad." I just want to get out of here, I hate hospitals.

"Good good. So your blood pressure has come down from when you came in. You went into hypertensive crisis, where essentially your blood pressure raises to such a high level that it made you lose consciousness. You got very lucky Mrs. Blackford. I have seen people rushed in with lower numbers than you that have had a stroke."

Fuck. A stroke? I know I've been stressed but enough to almost cause a stroke?

"Are you on any medication for high blood pressure?" He continues.

"No, I've never had high blood pressure before. How do I just go from being ok to being rushed into hospital?"

"Well it is possible your blood pressure has been on the higher side for a while. Things like unhealthy foods, alcohol, smoking and caffeine all have an effect on our blood pressure over time." Great, so everything I love I have to give up. Great.

"Stress is also a factor. When we get particularly stressed out our bodies release a large amount of adrenaline and cortisol, both of which cause your blood vessels to constrict, increasing your blood pressure. I understand you collapsed in a police station so can hazard a guess that you were more stressed than usual?"

"Uh, yeah, I guess you could say that."

"It is quite important that you try to remain as calm and relaxed as possible, for at least the next few days, so we don't have a repeat of this."

I can't help but laugh out loud!

"Ha!" He frowns at me. "Sorry I don't mean to be rude. My life is just a bit, uh, complicated at the moment."

"Well, you need to un-complicate it. Maybe try some meditation, or relaxing breathing?"

"Look, currently my husband, sorry, soon to be ex-husband is on the run after potentially killing a woman in my home, who he has been sleeping with, behind my back, for months. I have no access to any of our money because he has locked me out of all of our accounts, I am going to have to explain to my nine year old daughter not only why her parents aren't together anymore, but also why her Dad is in prison, and you are now telling me I can't smoke, eat crap or drink alcohol and coffee. I don't think relaxing breathing is going to do any good."

Everyone is quiet and the doctor's mouth is hanging open. I'm not sure if he is more stunned by my outburst or what I said.

Well that was rude.

"I'm sorry, I didn't mean to"- I start to apologise.

"No, please, I understand." He interrupts. He walks to the chair next to my bed and sits to look at me. "That really is an awful lot to deal with all in one go. I hope that you have a good support network at home? I know it's going to be particularly difficult with all you are going through, but you say you have a nine year old daughter?" I nod my head. "Then you must make sure you look after yourself above all so you can make sure you are around for her."

I know he is right. Stressing myself won't help the situation, it will only make me ill. Ami's father will no doubt end up in prison, she can't have her mother in and out of hospital too...

Or worse.

"Rachel?" Tad grabs one of my hands in both of his. "Why don't you come and stay with me? I have plenty of space, I have a spare room with an en suite, I've already taken the week off work, just come and stay with me so I can make sure you are resting."

We would definitely end up having sex all week, there would be nothing relaxing about it.

But it would be nicer than staying at my parents alone, and it would be much better for my back sleeping on a decent bed rather than a blow up mattress in a cramped office with three people sharing one bathroom.

The doctor stands.

"I'll leave you too it Mrs. Blackford. It looks like you will be well taken care of. I will get the nurses to get your medication sorted and once you have it and have signed your discharge papers you can go. Keep an eye on what you are eating, nothing high in cholesterol or saturated fats, watch out for the caffeine with chocolate, and just for now maybe switch to decaf."

I over exaggerate a shudder like I am disgusted and stick out my tongue like a stroppy child.

"Yuk, decaf. My life is over!"

"Just for a while until we get these numbers back down to where I am happy!" The doctor laughs, at least he has a good sense of humour, unlike some stuffy old so and so's I have seen here. "Book an appointment in with your GP for a few days' time to keep an eye on your BP, and for those few days, rest as much as you possibly can."

"Thank you very much Doctor."

He nods his head and walks out of the curtain.

"What is life with no coffee or chocolate or wine... or the occasional cigarette when I've had too much wine?" I'm half joking, but half not joking. It takes me about three cups of coffee of a morning to get me somewhere close to awake and then it keeps me going through the day until it is acceptable to drink wine.

"You are such a drama queen!" Celine laughs.

"If it's so easy to give up all of that stuff then you do it too!"

"Fine then, I will, no big deal." She will crumble after a few hours, I know her better than that.

"We will see!" I laugh at her. Tad stands up.

"I just need to quickly pop outside to make a call, I'll be back in a second. Rachel, please think about my offer." He smiles his gorgeous smile and his blue eyes have a twinkle in them that wasn't there when I first woke up. The butterflies start back up in my stomach again and I feel myself blush as I smile back at him. The effect he has on my body is ridiculous.

"You should stay with him." Celine has a soft smile on her face.

"Oh cheers, offer me a bed at yours and then tell me I'm suddenly not welcome!" I fake a hurt look and then smile at her.

"Look we both know my house isn't exactly very big, and I have honestly never seen you look as happy as you do when you are looking at him."

"But we have only just met. I don't really know anything about him. And"-

"Look you know his name, you have already seen each other naked, and babe, you told me you loved him. I don't really think at this point it matters how long you have known each other. Look at me and Dan, he told me he loved me after only knowing me a day and then proposed a week later! Everyone laughed at me, including you might I add!" She has a point, I told her they were both crazy and wouldn't last the month. I mouth the word sorry at her as she continues talking. "Look at us now, over a year down the line, living together, planning our wedding, planning a family.

Everything happens for a reason babe. You met him for a reason and you feel the way you do about him because you are supposed to. Yes he fucked up, but he is a man! It's what they do, but it's how they deal with their fuck ups that show you what they are really like, and he came running the second I called him. Plus he looked like a broken man when he burst through those curtains. You need to give him a chance. You deserve to be happy, and from everything you have told me, and from the way you look at each other, I think if anyone is going to give you the life you deserve it's going to be him."

My eyes sting with tears. How does this girl always know exactly what I need to hear?

"I love you Cel." I pull her in for a big hug.

"I love you too babe."

CHAPTER TWENTY FOUR

Tad

An hour later Rach has her medication, she has signed her discharge forms and she, Celine and I are in a cab on the way to Rachel's house. She needs to pick up some things and can't bear to go inside, which is understandable so Celine said she would go and grab some bits for her. As we turn into her road we see there are two police cars outside her house and a stream of officers walking in and out. Well this isn't going to be helping her stress levels at all. I look at her and she looks pale.

"Hey," I take my hand and gently pull her face to look at mine. "Just breathe, everything will be fine, I promise." She smiles softly at me and puts her hand on the side of my face. Tingles run all over my body when she touches me, it just feels so right.

"I'm going to have to speak to them aren't I?" She is still smiling at me but her eyes betray how scared she really is.

"Let's just go and see if there is any update okay? I'll come with you." She closes her eyes and nods at me.

"Do you think they will let me in to get some bits for you?" Celine is looking around at all of the police out of the window and is biting her nails again.

"I'll speak to them first and see what they say." Rachel turns to smile at her too.

"Please wait here." I hand the driver a fifty and get out of the car. I walk around and open the front door for Celine and door behind for Rachel. I take her hand and help her out of the car.

We walk over to the house and Rachel squeezes my hand as she seems to recognize someone.

"That's DC Robins, he is in charge of the case." We walk towards him and he turns and walks over to Rachel when he sees her.

"Mrs. Blackford, you're looking much better. I'm surprised to see you out of hospital though." He seems genuinely concerned. He is an older gentleman, with a very kind face. Doesn't look half mean enough to be in the police.

"Please, call me Rachel. I'm ok, just a bit of high blood pressure that's all. Sorry I caused such a scene!"

"Well I'm pleased you are better now." He looks towards Rachel's house. "I'm so sorry about all of this. We have a warrant if you would like to see it, but we needed to search the property and get forensics to have a look around. I hope you understand?"

Rachel's eyes glaze over. This must be such a lot to take in for her. I can't even imagine what she is going through. She slowly nods her head.

"Would it be possible for us to collect some clothes and things for Rachel?" I ask. I don't think she has the strength to speak, and I need her to stay strong and calm.

"Yes, of course that won't be an issue. I will have to have someone escort you though and just check what it is you are taking. Procedure I'm afraid."

Rachel just nods again and takes a deep breath in.

"Is it ok for my friend to go in? I don't think I can face going in there right now."

"Yes of course, I will go and find an officer to take you around, be back in a mo."

"I loved that house." Rachel lets out a long sigh. Celine puts a reassuring arm around Rachel, and she leans her head into her.

"I know you did babe."

They stand in silence for a few minutes until Robins comes back with a young officer.

"This is Lucy. She will take you around the house."

Celine kisses the top of Rachel's head and walks off into the house with Lucy.

I take over where Celine left off and wrap my arm around Rachel. She turns into me and wraps her arms around my waist. I pull her close into me and feel something just click into place.

"How long have you known Celine?" I run my fingers through her beautifully soft hair.

"Most of my life, we went to primary school together."

"She's a wonderful friend."

"She is the best."

Robins starts to walk back over to us.

"So sorry to bother you again Rachel, but we still haven't heard anything from Kevin and we have no idea where he is. Just a heads up that we are going to have to issue a statement for the press asking that if anyone has seen him they call us. I know you have a young daughter and I am so sorry it has to come to this, but maybe try to keep her away from the television for a few days at least."

"She is staying in a caravan with my parents for the week so hopefully she should avoid it. But I'm going to have to tell her something aren't I."

I can see a panicked look spread across her face.

"Don't worry about that for today. Look at me," I grab her chin with my hand and make her look at me in the eyes. "We will work out what to tell her and it will all be fine. Maybe not straight away, but I promise, kids are resilient, and if Amelia is anything like her mum she will be strong too."

She smiles at me, closes her eyes and exhales deeply.

CHAPTER TWENTY FIVE

An hour later we are back at my house. Rachel is curled up on my sofa with a blanket watching some crappy show on the telly and I've come upstairs to run her a nice bath in my whirlpool tub. I've just finished an online shop, and ordered all sorts of healthy foods. Fresh fruit and vegetables, lean meats, and a ton of decaf coffee.

I've made up the spare room for her. As much as I want her to sleep in my bed with me, I know that I need to prove to her that I am a gentleman and I need to show her some respect and a little self-control. So we are going to do this properly and slowly, and take our time. In reality we have only known each other for two days. That's it, two. We have already skipped getting to know each other and first dates and straight away got to sleeping together and now living together.

I go downstairs and sit next to her on the sofa. She lays down and rests her head on my lap.

"Thank you." I say as I stroke her soft hair.

She looks slightly confused.

"For what?"

"For giving me a second chance, and for letting me look after you."

She looks up at me and smiles.

"Who said I'm giving you a second chance? I just didn't want to sleep on a bouncy castle at Cel's!" She winks at me and giggles. She looks so much more relaxed than earlier. I love it when she smiles.

"Well in that case I will just go and get in the luxurious bubble bath I just ran for you, myself."

"Hmm. Maybe I can give you a second chance then...?" She grins at me. I stand up and make my way to the stairs.

"Did I mention it was a Jacuzzi?"

"Yep, definitely got a second chance, now get out of the way I have a Jacuzzi to jump in." I chuckle as I watch her race up the stairs. My heart feels like it is hurting, not in a bad way, but in an *'I can't believe it took me so long to find you'*, kind of way. She is honestly the most amazing person I have ever met and I can't imagine what she must have gone through over the last few years.

I go upstairs and knock on my bathroom door.

"What are you knocking for?" She asks amused.

"Just trying to be a gentleman." I grin. I walk through the door to see her standing in just her bra and knickers. She truly is stunning. I take a seat on the edge of my bath and just stare at her.

"A gentleman wouldn't stare at a young scantily clad lady."

"Well maybe being a gentleman isn't for me." I laugh. She smiles at me and removes her bra and underwear effortlessly, and walks towards me.

Gosh I want to just bend her over and fuck her right here. She knows that too and she is obviously teasing me. I hold my hand out to help her into the bath.

"Oh my god that is amazing!" She says as she sits and I turn the bubbles on. She lays back and closes her eyes.

I could watch her like this for hours. Relaxed and beautiful, laying back with her beautiful breasts just peeping out above the water. I feel my cock stir and realise I need to make myself scarce before I can't stop myself.

"Can I get you anything?"

"How about a glass of wine?" She grins at me.

"I will rephrase. Can I get you anything you are actually allowed to have?"

"You spoil sport." She splashes water in my direction. "Just some juice or something then as I can't even have a coffee. And hey, you aren't allowed any coffee either while I'm here!"

"No problem. I have all I need here anyway." I kiss her on the head and go downstairs to the kitchen.

Rachel

I swear this is a magic bathtub. The jets of hot bubbles are actually melting away every single one of my problems. All I can think about it this bath! And the man that the bath belongs too. And the fact that I am free now. Once all of this comes out Kevin will almost certainly end up in prison. There is evidence of him assaulting me. That's reasonable grounds for divorce right there, and given what is happening right now, I can't see a court giving him custody if he somehow avoids prison. It would be supervised visits in a contact centre.

I'm free.

I'm free.

Of course telling Amelia is going to be absolutely awful. He has been a good enough father to her, and I know how cruel kids can be. The thought of her being bullied because of what her Dad did hurts me. But Tad is right, kids really are resilient. We can move away if we need to. Start a fresh. Although I really hope it doesn't come to that because I really, *really* want to stay close to Tad.

I'm going to have to call my parents in a minute and let them know what is going on. That is not going to be a fun conversation.

I hear footsteps and Tad appears in the doorway with a glass of orange juice.

His smile has pretty much the same effect on me as these bubbles do. All my troubles just seems to stop existing when he catches my eye and smiles like that at me.

"What are you thinking about?" I ask him.

"How great your tits look like that." He winks at me and comes to sit on the side of the bath.

I frown at him.

"Really? That's definitely not very gentleman like!"

"Ok, no not really! I'm just thinking how completely crazy this weekend has been. And how I am so *so* incredibly lucky that I met you, and one day I will need to thank someone."

My smile must look sickening, but I can't control it. I feel exactly the same about him.

I love you Tad.

We are both staring in each other's eyes and the sexual tension in the room is insane. I can feel myself start to throb and out the corner of my eye I'm sure I can see something stirring under his trousers.

I push myself up so I am sitting and turn off the bubbles. He is watching every movement I make, his eyes not straying from mine. I run my tongue over my bottom lip, and see something flash in his eyes. He blinks, stands up and says he is going to get me some towels.

What was that? Fuck the towels, I could happily air dry or use his body to dry me off. Or he could have got in the bath with me, it's definitely big enough!

I sit frustrated and wait for him to come back. He is carrying my phone.

"Before you say anything, I wasn't snooping. I didn't answer it, but I heard it buzzing on the table so ran to get it for you. It was your dad but I didn't get back up here before it cut to voicemail."

"Thank you. I guess I should call him and let him know what is going on. Can I really not have wine?"

"I can nip out and get you some non-alcoholic stuff if you'd like?"

I just stare at him stone faced. I think he gets the message.

"Um I will take that as a no then?" He puts the towels and my phone down, and grabs my hands in his. "I'm not trying to be an arse, but I want you better. I was absolutely terrified today. I thought you were going to die." Oh god, his eyes are watering. My heart hurts. "Celine said you looked like you'd had a heart attack..." He closes his eyes. "My brother died, only a few weeks ago, from a heart attack, caused by a congenital condition that we didn't know about until it was too late. When Celine called I thought it was happening all over again. I just lost my brother then I meet this amazing woman who manages to make me feel happy again, I fuck things up with her and then before I have a chance to fix things..." He tails off as if it's just too much for him to think about, let alone speak about. I quickly stand and get out of the bath, wrap a towel around myself then pull him up into my arms.

"I'm so sorry Tad. I had no idea. Today must have been absolutely awful for you. I can't even imagine what you must be going through. But I am here and I am ok. And I'm not going anywhere you hear? Well unless you want me to that is."

He kisses the top of my head.

"Why on earth would I ever want you to go anywhere?"

We stand, locked in an embrace for a long few minutes. A buzzing from my feet interrupts us and I see my Dad is calling again.

Oh God.

"Good luck!" Tad says. "I'll go and make us something to eat."

He kisses my cheek and walks downstairs.

Reluctantly, I answer the phone.

"Hey Daddy."

"Hi princess, any news?"

"Uh. Yeah. Dad, where's Ami?"

"She is outside with your mum. She's made a few friends with some other kids staying here."

"That's nice..."

"For God sake Rachel, it can't be that bad."

I sit down on the edge of the bath and brace myself.

"Ok, I don't really know how to put any of this so just bear with me. So Friday night, Kevin and I went to a fundraiser in London. He had far too much to drink and accused me with flirting with a guy at our table, then he tried to attack me"–

"He did WHAT?"

"Dad please, there are going to be lots of things you are going to want to scream about, but we will be here all night. Make notes if you need to, but let me get through this."

"Sorry. Go on."

"So um, he went home and I stayed at the hotel all night. I got home the next morning and he had completely trashed the house, and then he accused me of sleeping with the guy at the fundraiser. He was still wasted, he must have been drinking all night. He slapped me and I ran out and went to a friend's house. I went home later that evening and saw load of police at the park behind the house. I bumped into someone Kevin works with and he mentioned he had been at the house this morning and Kevin said I was in bed, so I just corrected him and said Kevin must have been mistaken as I stayed out by myself last night." I stop to take a breath.

"My brain hurts, is there much more?"

"Sorry Dad, this isn't the half of it... So I go back to the house with a plan to stay with Celine if he's still in and drunk. Turns out the house is spotless and he is inside cooking me a romantic dinner, flowers and all. After we've eaten he basically slips in the conversation that he needs me to lie and say I was with him all night. I tell him about already seeing his colleague and saying he must have been confused and he loses his shit, starts throwing plates, grabs me. It was awful." Tears prick at my eyes at the memory of it all. "Anyway, I managed to kick him in the balls then ran off. I got a phone call from the police this morning, they needed to see me. It turns out that they found a body behind our house. The body of a woman Kevin has been sleeping with for the past few months. The body of a woman who Kevin picked up in the cab on the way back to our house on Friday."

Silence.

"He is now missing, the police can't get hold of him and are having to do a press release tomorrow to ask that anyone who sees him or knows where he is contacts the police."

I try to give my Dad a moment to process all of this.

"Dad?"

"Yeah. Fuck." My Dad never ever swears. "This is a stupid question, but are you ok?"

"Um, I had a bit of an episode this morning with a bit of high blood pressure. I'm fine now, on tablets and told to rest as a precaution though. I'm just worried about how Amelia is going to handle this."

"Yeah, that's going to be a whole lot of information for her to take on. Poor kiddo."

"Dad don't, its breaking me."

"Kevin has always been like this hasn't he?"

"No, not always, and never quite this bad." I can hear Ami laughing in the background.

"Dad, tell Mum by all means, but please don't let Ami watch the news or go on Facebook, just for a few days. I know it's extremely unlikely but this could all be a misunderstanding and I don't want her to be told unless necessary."

"Of course sweetheart. Wanna say hello?"

I hear him pass the phone over.

"Mummy! I am having the best ever time! The caravan is so cool, I made Nanny and Gramps stay in it last night even though it was still on their drive. I fell out of my bed, cause it's so small, but I'm ok now! And we went straight to the arcade when we got here and I won the jackpot on one of the machines Mum! Two thousand tickets! I'm saving up and I'm going to get a giant teddy bear with all my winnings!"

"Wow you sound like you're having a great time! And Gramps said you made some friends?"

"I did Mum, I went to the club after lunch and everyone is so nice. I love it here, can we come back soon, and can you come next time, because I really miss you Mummy."

"I miss you too baby. We will definitely go back, just you, me, Nanny and Gramps, sound good?"

"Yeah! Love you Mum. I have to go my friends are calling me! Love you."

She hangs the phone up and I debate calling my Dad back. He probably needs a bit of time to process everything that I told him, so I just text him instead.

I know that was a lot to take in, so I will leave you to it for tonight and give you a call tomorrow. Thank you so much for taking such good care of Ami. Please don't worry about me, I'm being looked after well. Love you loads Daddy xx

I wander out of the bathroom and into the spare bedroom that Tad has made up for me. It is beautiful, the carpet is so soft I want to just lay on it! Everything is cream, and clean looking. There is a huge bed in the middle of the room with a gold headboard, cream bedding and about ten cream and gold pillows. In front of the window is a beautiful cream and gold chaise longue. It feels absolutely luxurious. But I find myself wondering why he has set me up in my own room? We have already slept together, and as I am here and now practically single I'd quite like to make the most of the time we spend together. But he is pulling away from me when I want him and has set me up in a room away from him. But then he just told me how glad he is he met me? My brain hurts. I am just going to have to take this as it comes. I have no idea what *normal* is when starting a relationship, or whatever this is.

I have been with Kevin since I was sixteen! I hadn't even dated really before him, I'd had a couple of cheeky snogs round the back of the bike sheds at school, but that's as much real life experience as I have. Even with Kevin, things were boring and stale from very early on, we never really kissed or showed any affection to each other. And honestly I don't even remember the last time we had sex. I do know Ami was still very small. Sex with Kevin was always a chore. I only did it because he made a point that married couples should have sex. It was always boring. I used to go in search of my sexual kicks elsewhere, from books to films. In the beginning I always used to try to spice things up, but he was never interested.

I didn't even know sex existed like the sex I had with Tad. It was on completely another level. He has a look in his eyes that says to me that he is far more willing to act out my deepest darkest fantasies. I feel my stomach flutter and my sex clench at the though. His voice interrupts my sordid thoughts as he shouts up the stairs.

"Rachel, food is almost done."

I reluctantly stand up and walk over to the window where Tad has put my bags. I open them up and laugh as I start to look through what Celine has packed me.

That woman!

Inside are some of the skimpiest items I own. Lacy underwear sets, stockings and suspender belts, satin PJs and dressing gown. I open the other bag to see tops with plunging necklines, tiny skirts and shorts and ridiculously skinny jeans. I had forgotten I owned half of this stuff, I haven't worn it in years and I doubt most of it still fits! Must remind myself to call Celine later and ask her what the hell she was thinking!

For now I decide to take advantage. I pull out the deep purple satin pyjamas and dressing gown. The top is a little vest top with spaghetti straps, and the bottoms are very short shorts with slits right up the sides of the legs. The dressing gown barley covers my bum and I leave it open.

I quickly shake my hair out and make my way downstairs.

CHAPTER TWENTY SIX

Tad

I shouldn't really be trusted in a kitchen, but I figured pasta with some chicken and a tomato sauce out of a jar would be easy enough. It smells ok, the pasta is soft and the chicken has no pink bits, so I think it's ok. I'm just about to start slicing through some crusty bread when I turn my head and see Rachel stood in the doorway looking fucking stunning. I completely stop what I am doing and the impulse to pick her up and bend her over the kitchen counter is almost too much to bear.

"Woah." I can't even speak coherently.

Her cheeks flush red and she smiles nervously at me.

"I think Celine may have had some sort of ulterior motive when packing my stuff. This is one of the less revealing things she packed."

"Please remind me to thank Celine when I next see her." I meant it as a joke, but there is no humour in my voice. I can't stop staring at her and I can feel my boxers getting tighter.

"You like then?" She runs a hand down her stomach on to her leg and bites her bottom lip. She does that on purpose now. She knows it drives me crazy and she is deliberately teasing me.

I try to talk, but instead a low growl comes out of my mouth. Fuck I'm so turned on I can't think straight.

No sex. No sex the doctor said when I ran out to ask him. Well sort of. But she is supposed to be resting!

She slowly walks over to me and gives me a peck on the cheek before sitting at one of the stools next to me.

"What are we eating then?"

Oh I wish I was eating you.

"Uh I threw together some chicken and pasta. I told you, cooking isn't my strong point."

"Well it smells gorgeous."

"So do you." I wink at her. I think I can start to function normally again now that I can't see half of her.

"Can I help?"

"You are supposed to be resting, so make the most of me waiting on you hand and foot for the next few days."

"I feel loads better now, I think that bath fixed my blood pressure to be honest. It's amazing."

"Well still, Doctors orders!"

"Are you always this bossy?" She looks playfully at me.

"Only when needed!" I grin at her.

I get some plates out of a cupboard, and a ready-made salad out of the fridge. I put some pasta and salad on a plate and then cut two thick slices of bread.

We eat in relative silence, but the atmosphere is thick with lust.

"That really was good Tad, thank you." Rachel has cleared her plate and takes it over to the sink with mine. "You sure you aren't a secret chef?"

I laugh.

"No, definitely not a chef!"

"What is it you do then?"

"It's a bit long and complicated, but short version; I go through the markets and look out for businesses that are failing and on the verge of collapse. I have a look at the company and see if there is anything obvious that needs changing, or doing, or if I know of a similar company that could merge with the failing one to keep it going. If I think it is worth my while I buy the business at a reasonable price, do as much as I can do to either get it back on track, or merge it with another company, either one of my own or one I have sold before, and then I sell it for quite a bit more than I bought it for."

"So, you take things that are broken and fix them? A bit like you did with me?"

Hmm, I had never thought of it like that.

"I suppose in a way." I laugh. "One big difference though."

I go to the fridge and pull out two non-alcoholic beers that have been hiding from last Christmas.

"What's that then?"

"There is no way in hell I am letting you go anywhere."

I put the beers on the counter top and look across to see Rachel smiling at me. I smile back at her and find the bottle opener in the drawer.

I open our drinks and pour them in two glasses.

"Just pretend it has alcohol in it." I say as I hand it to a disgusted looking Rachel. "It's really not that bad!"

"I feel like I am cheating on alcohol."

"You aren't cheating, you're on a break. Alcohol will understand."

"Uh did you watch Friends?"

We both laugh.

She takes a cautious sip.

"Actually you wouldn't know it doesn't have alcohol in it. Does the non-boozy wine taste the same as boozy wine then?"

"Not sure, never had it. We can go out and get some tomorrow if you want?"

A couple of hours later and we are cuddled up on the sofa watching Love Actually. Apparently its one of Rachel's favourite films. I know we have done this a bit backwards, but we've spent most of the last hour just chatting about our lives. It feels so nice to get to know more about her.

"Tad?"

"Yeah?"

"Why have you set me up in the spare room?"

"Well I just thought you might like your own space. And I know that things have already moved lightning fast between us, but I wondered if maybe we should slow things down a bit? Get to know each other more? I really like you Rachel. I don't want this to get so hot so fast that it burns out. Is that ok?"

She sits up and turns to look at me.

"Of course that is ok, but that sort of leads me to my next awkward question..."

"Go on...?"

"Well what is this? What are we doing? I know my life is ridiculously messed up right now and I have enough baggage to take down a 747, so if all you want is something more casual, that's fine, but I need to know."

"I don't think I can do casual with you Rachel. I don't know what you have done to me." I gently stroke her hair behind her ear. "I've never been in a proper relationship before because I've never felt, well, this. So I guess what I am saying is I want to give this a real go. Baggage and all."

She leans in and presses her lips gently against mine. My eyes close instinctively and I brush my hand gently through her hair. Her lips slowly move against mine, and I gently push my tongue through her lips and brush it softly against hers. She makes a little sigh and it takes everything in me to not pick her up and carry her up to bed.

My cock is completely unimpressed by my holding back and feels like it is trying to escape in protest. She runs her hand down my back, around my thigh and leaves it dangerously close to the hard bulge in my trousers. I quickly pull back and hold her away.

"Listen," I clear my throat, "um, I sort of asked the doctor if it was ok for you to have sex." Her eyes shoot open wide and her mouth opens in a half shocked, half amused grin.

"He said that sex does temporarily increase blood pressure, so to go slow for a few days until your blood pressure is back to normal."

Rachel looks like she doesn't know whether to laugh or slap me. Eventually she laughs.

"I cannot believe you asked him that! Well, let's go slow then..." She pushes back into me and starts to kiss me again.

"Oh Rach, baby." I try to speak as she keeps kissing me. "I don't think I could go slow with you. We should just hold off for a few days."

She pulls back and slowly stands. She starts speaking as she lowers herself onto my lap, straddling me with both her knees either side of my legs.

"I have had to give up wine, coffee and chocolate. I can just about deal with that. But there is no way in hell I am giving up you."

She wiggles herself forwards until I can feel the heat from her pussy over my rock hard cock.

I deserve a fucking medal for the amount of self-restraint I am showing right now.

"But Rach"-

"Besides, we can't possibly leave you in this state." Her hands run down my stomach and onto the waistband of my trousers. I know I should stop her but this feels so good.

She lifts her hips and pulls down my trousers. My cock has found an escape out of the front opening of my pants, I look at Rachel's face as she is staring at me. She licks her lips and bites that damned bottom lip again. She runs her hand back up over my thigh and grabs hold of my head, as she squeezes it, a bead of clear pre come spills out of me. I close my eyes and groan.

"You aren't going to take no for an answer are you?" I ask her in a low voice.

"I'm not a monster Tad, if you really don't want to fuck me, just say the word and I will just suck your beautiful cock instead."

Oh my God, she is the perfect woman.

"It's not that I don't want to fuck you, and you know it, but Doctors orders you know." I grin at her and she smiles a filthy smile at me.

"Have it your way then."

She shuffles back on my lap, stands up, grabs hold of my boxers and pulls them down and off in one swift movement. She pushes my legs apart and lowers herself in between them.

She wraps her hand around me and squeezes so that more pre come beads out of the top. She moves her hand up and rubs her thumb over the tip, she starts to work the top of my cock with her hand and it feels so fucking good. I look at her and she is looking me straight in the eye. Slowly, and never losing eye contact, she lowers her head and gently takes me in her mouth. I can't look away from her, watching her move her head down and take almost all of me in her mouth and throat. She holds me there for a moment until she comes back up, panting. She grips her hand around the base of my hard on and starts to gently suck me. In and out of her mouth as her hand works me from the bottom. My hips start to thrust along with her and my hands grab fistfuls of her hair. It doesn't take long before a familiar feeling starts creeping over me and I know I am about to explode into her mouth. What the fuck does this woman do to me? Nobody has ever made me come the way she does.

"Ah Rach, I'm gonna come."

She starts moving faster and sucking harder.

"Ah fuck! Yes!" I hiss as I feel my whole body tense up. Suddenly I feel my whole body let go as I feel the first burst of my come shoot into the back of her throat. She slows down and gently keeps pumping me while more come shoots out of me in steady spurts. She sucks every drop from me. I slump back panting. She takes me out of her mouth and kisses my thighs.

"Jesus Rachel."

She stands up and puts her head on my chest as she sits next to me.

"Rach?"

"Yes babe?"

"The Doctor only said no sex..."

She lifts her head to look at me.

"What are you thinking?"

Without a word I push her back onto the sofa and start kissing her. Her hands are in my hair and her kiss is frantic and desperate. I start to move lower, kissing her neck, and then the tops of her breasts. I drop to my knees and push her leg around me so I am in between her.

I gently pull her top down so that her beautiful tits are exposed. I run my fingertips from the bottom of her neck, down to her hard nipples and I squeeze each of them gently.

She bites her lip.

"You don't have to be so gentle with me you know?"

I squeeze harder and she moans and arches her back.

"Mmmm, you like it rough then?" I start trailing kisses up the inside of her thighs.

"God yes."

Never let her go. She is perfect.

"Hmm, I will remember that then."

I trace my hands down her top until I get to the top of her tiny shorts. I hook my thumbs around the top and pull down. She slightly lifts her hips as I slide them off and throw them over my shoulder.

"I don't think I will ever get tired of seeing your beautiful pussy."

I lean in and gently start to kiss around her, barley touching her.

She grips the sofa hard and whimpers.

"Stop being such a tease!"

"I want you to lift your legs up on the sofa, as wide apart as you can, and to hold them there. Ok?"

Without a word she lifts her legs and reveals even more of her soft pink flesh, soaking wet and ready for me. She grabs hold of her legs and looks at me hungrily.

"Don't move your hands or legs ok? Or I will stop."

Fuck this is so hot. I wish I could pound her into the middle of next week.

She nods her head slowly. I scratch gently down the inside of her legs, from her knees right down to her beautiful arse. Her whole body jolts.

I lean in and as my tongue touches her clit she lets out a long breathy moan. I gently start to lick and suck her. My cock is already rock hard and standing to attention in between my legs and all I want to do is thrust it into her. I make do with two fingers instead. God her pussy is so tight. I slowly move them in and out of her, she is so wet her juices are spilling out of her. Her breathing is fast and heavy. I start to move my fingers harder and faster.

"Oh yes!" she cries out.

I start to suck and lick her harder as I gently slip another finger inside of her.

"Aah fuck!" She screams in pleasure.

My little finger is dangerously close to her arsehole. I so want to explore that, and every part of her, but not today.

I push my fingers into her as deep as I can and start to massage her G spot.

The noises she is making have made me hard again. With my free hand I grab hold of my cock and try to make it behave.

She starts to arch her chest and I know she is close. I start licking her in a frenzy, hard and fast as I pump her inside. Her hips lift off the sofa as she screams out.

"Fuck! Yes! Oh Tad!"

Her body starts shaking, her breathing is loud and ragged, her cheeks and chest flush a beautiful shade of red. She cries out and I can feel her pulsating as she comes hard. She is so tight she almost crushes my fingers. The sensation of it all is too much and I can't stop myself. I pull my fingers out and stand over her beautiful body, still twitching from her orgasm. My fingers are soaked with her come, and I grab hold of my cock and start to wank over her. It only takes a few pumps of my fist before I am exploding all over her stomach.

Rachel

oly shit that was hot.

Tad is standing over me, cock in his hand, with the last of his come spilling from him.

I look up at his face and his eyes are closed. He opens them and looks straight at me, a slight smile creeping over his face.

"Sorry. You're just so hot I couldn't help myself."

"No need to apologise. Watching you jerk off actually happens to be a hobby of mine."

He looks confused.

Shit! Idiot! He doesn't know you perved on him!

He sits down next to me and looks at me.

"Huh?"

"Fuck." I put my hands over my face to cover my embarrassment.

"Rach?" I can hear him grinning.

"Don't get mad?" I say from behind my hands.

"I won't!" He thinks this is funny.

He won't when he knows what a weirdo you are!

"Well, you know when I came round yesterday afternoon and you went for a shower?"

He stays silent.

Fuck.

I move one of my fingers and peek through to see his face. His mouth is open but he is definitely half smiling.

"I am such a pervert! I'm sorry!"

His face breaks into a huge grin and he starts to laugh.

"So you watched me, in the shower?"

"Yeah. I didn't mean to. I just wanted to see you, naked, because I'm an absolute pervert. Oh God!"

His laughter is infectious and it sets me off.

"Stop laughing! It's not funny!" I try to say through my giggles.

"Is that why you ran off?"

"Well, yeah! When I realised what you were doing I tried to go downstairs before I saw too much, but I swear my feet just refused to move, and my eyes too for that matter. And then when I finally managed to peel myself off of your doorframe I knew that I had to leave or I would jump you the second I saw you. Hence why I did jump you the second I saw you."

"Oh my God Rachel! Well, as it is such a hobby of yours I'll be sure to do it more often then."

He winks at me and I feel myself blush.

He stands up.

"I'll just go and get a towel for you and then we can go and have a shower. No more shows for tonight though I'm afraid baby, I'm spent!"

A little while later we are both showered, dressed, and laying on my bed in the spare room.

Tad is tracing a pattern on the palm of my hand and I can feel myself drifting off to sleep.

"I'm so pleased you're here Rach baby."

"Mmmm me too." I mumble, half asleep.

"I'll stay here until you're sleeping, ok?"

"Mmhmm."

I feel him kiss me on the head.

"Goodnight baby."

CHAPTER TWENTY SEVEN

I wake up to the sounds of birds tweeting away outside of my window. I feel like I've slept for weeks. I don't think I have ever slept as well as I do when I am here.

My heart sinks a little at the realisiaton that I am in the bed alone. Tad obviously went back into his bed once I fell asleep. I shuffle around in bed to look at the clock on the wall, 10.30am. I don't remember the last time I slept in this late. Something on the bedside table catches my eye, a folded piece of paper with my name on it. A huge smile lights up my face.

Good morning baby,

I hope you slept well. I'll be in my office when you wake up. Come and get me and I will make you breakfast.

Tad xx

P.s. Do you know you sleep talk?

Sleep talk?

Oh shit!

I wonder what I said?!

He has laid out my little satin dressing gown and some slippers next to the bed for me, so I put them on and wander off downstairs.

As I'm walking down the stairs I realise I don't even know where his office is. There is a door under the stairs, which looks like it could lead to a cellar or something. I doubt that is his office. And then I hear voices.

"I do understand Jeff, but there comes a point where you just need to cut your losses. If you carry on the way you are going you will be broke within a year. You won't have enough money for redundancy pay for any of your staff, so they will be fucked. You will not only be ruining your career and life, but those of everyone who works for you. It's a huge price to pay for pride."

It's not Tad speaking, the voice sounds tinny and is echoing so I assume it is coming from a phone or computer. "Look, I know it will be at a loss, but you sell to us for five and a half mil and that's five and a half mil in your pocket. You have no redundancy pay to worry about, no outstanding bills to pay up, just enough money to happily settle down and retire."

"And then what about all my staff? What about the name I have built up for myself?" Another voice starts speaking. "I know that Turner is ruthless. If he doesn't think my company is worth his time then he will just dissolve everything. And then none of my staff have jobs anyway."

I wonder if he knows Tad is listening? But seriously, my Tad, ruthless? Doesn't sound like him at all! I start to walk towards the door at the other side of the kitchen where the voices are coming from.

"Mr. Turner is confident that with some re branding and merging some aspects of one of his own companies that we will be able to clear all the companies outstanding debt and keep on at least 90% of current staffing. Anyone who we aren't able to keep will either be offered a job in another of our companies if there are any suitable openings, or given a very generous amount for redundancy."

"And Turner wouldn't be willing to buy half and leave me as partner?"

"You know that is not how we do business Harris."

"This guy is doing my fucking head in Scott. Tell him to take it or fuck off. I'm fed up of his shit."

That was definitely Tad's voice, but I have never heard him speak like that. He's so gentle when he is around me. He seems so kind, like he'd never raise his voice at anyone. Maybe work Tad is ruthless. Maybe he puts on some big, angry, money hungry persona. I suppose you don't make millions by being a nice guy.

An image of me bent over a desk with Tad in a power suit flashes through my brain and makes my stomach flip.

I get to the door and it is already open most of the way. I can see Tad sitting at a desk. He is wearing a tight fitting white t shirt that clings to his hard chest, his hair is messy and his stubble is starting to look a little untidy. But God he looks gorgeous. He looks totally engrossed in his computer, and he looks stressed. Or angry I'm not sure really, but the only other time I've seen him looking a little like this was at the hotel when he pulled Kevin off of me.

I very lightly tap the door, not wanting to disturb his phone call.

He turns to look at me. His whole demeanor changes and his face immediately softens.

The two other voices are still in a heated discussion.

"Hey beautiful. Oh shit Scott not you, I'm off for now. Call me back when this stubborn arsehole has made up his mind." He pushes a button on is phone and turns back to look at me. His blue eyes are sparkling at me. He really is stunning.

"Morning." I start to wander over to his desk, my brain flashing back to the thoughts of him doing me over it...

"How did you sleep?" He grabs my hand as soon as I get close to him and pulls me down on his lap. I wrap my arm around his shoulders and nuzzle my face into his neck. He smells so good, no real specific smell, just him. If I could bottle that I would be a rich woman.

"Better than I have in ages. How about you?"

"I couldn't really sleep. Felt odd that you were next door instead of with me."

"Then why didn't you get in with me?" I look up at him and kiss him gently on the lips.

His eyes glint and he smirks at me.

"I did, but you kept me up!"

Uh oh. The sleep talking.

"Oh, yeah. I didn't know I talked in my sleep. Dare I ask what I said?"

"What were you dreaming about Rach?" He smooths a strand of hair behind my ear sending tingles throughout my entire body.

Shit, what was I dreaming about?!

"Uhh I don't remember...!" I can feel myself blushing, his smile is getting bigger, but slightly darker. I can't really read his face.

"Can you just tell me what I said please, I'm worried now!"

He moves his mouth right next to my ear, so close I can feel his lips brushing against my skin, and he starts to whisper softly in my ear.

"I think you might have been having a dirty dream." The sensation of his lips and his warm breath tickling my ear are sending tingles everywhere and making my insides clench. I can feel myself growing hot, and I close my eyes as I desperately try to re ground myself. "Like to be tied up do you dirty girl?"

Oh fuck! My cheeks flash read, but I'm not sure if it is from embarrassment or being so turned on right now. He nips my ear suddenly and pulls back. My ear suddenly feels cold and I want to pull him back and make him carry on.

"So do you?" He asks again.

"I wouldn't know, but I'd love to try it."

His face suddenly looks shocked.

"You've never been tied up before?" He says, the tone of surprise in his voice is unmistakable.

"I told you, it's been a very *very* long time since I had any kind of sex. Kevin was my first, and to be honest he was the most boring lay I could ever imagine. Even in the beginning before everything turned to utter shit, I would ask if we could try things and he would shoot me down. Honestly, before you the most exciting sex I ever had was on my sofa."

"You have got to be joking?" Tad looks half amused and half horrified.

"No!" I laugh. "Genuinely I think I have had sex less than ten times in my life, and two of those times were with you."

Tad's mouth hangs open in mock horror.

"Oh Rach!" He pulls me closer to him and starts stroking my face. "So, what were these things you've always wanted to do then?"

My cheeks flash with heat again and I know this time it's embarrassment. Celine sort of knows some of my fantasies because, well she is my best friend, and when you're drunk with your best friend and not getting any sex, what's better to do than talk about all the sex you wish you were getting! But she doesn't know all of it, and even with what she knows she thinks I am a little crazy! I'm scared I will end up terrifying Tad if I tell him all my deep, dark little kinks.

"Uhh, well being tied up is one." I start chewing nervously on my lip.

"Well I know that one, and I would be more than happy to oblige." His eyes flash with that familiar look that tells me he wants me.

"You would?" I feel slightly less nervous that he is at least a little on my wavelength.

"Fuck Rach. The thought of you tied up and helpless, and me doing whatever I wanted to you..." He trails off and I start to feel him stiffen under my legs. My eyes widen and I can feel myself getting wetter by the second.

"That is definitely one of my fantasies right there. Tied, gagged, blindfolded, and totally vulnerable." He is rock hard underneath me now and I can hear his breath has started to quicken.

Maybe he is just as fucked up as me!

"So, you like the idea of someone else taking control then?"

"Not someone else Tad, you. I didn't think I would ever trust anyone enough to put myself in that position with them. And I know it's completely crazy because we have only just met, but when you know, you know right?"

Tad

Where the fuck has this woman been all my life. She is actually perfect for me in every single way. God the thought of her all tied up and completely at my mercy is enough to send me crazy. The fact she trusts me enough to be the one she wants to share this with after such a short time is making my stomach do somersaults. Well it's either that or the general thoughts in my head at the moment.

Without a word I lunge forward, almost pushing her off my lap and kiss her with such force I hear her struggle to catch her breath. My hands are running through her hair and down her back as my lips are all over hers. She throws her hands into my hair and kisses me back as if her life depends on it. She suddenly pulls away from my lips and puts them next to my ear and starts to whisper.

"Being tied up is probably the most vanilla of all my fantasies Tad."

Fuck. She's gonna make me explode without even touching me if she carries on.

"Tell me." I stare at her. Her cheeks blush as if she is embarrassed.

There is honestly very little I wouldn't happily do to her, she has no need at all to be embarrassed.

I grab her hair, slightly rougher than before and pull her head back, exposing her neck to my lips. I trail kisses from her collar bone up to her ear.

"Tell me baby." I whisper in her ear. Her breathing starts to speed up and I can feel goosebumps all over her neck.

"Uh, well..." She clears her throat as if trying to sound a little more confident. "How do you feel about spanking?"

"Mmmm." Is the only sound I can manage to make. I am having to try extremely hard to control myself at the moment. I don't think the things that I want to do to this goddess right now would do her high blood pressure any good at all.

I trail my kisses further down until I am at the top of her breasts, I pull down her little satin vest top and run my tongue all the way down to her nipple, I wrap my lips around it and gently suck. She tightens her grip in my hair and lets out a husky moan. I bite her nipple hard.

"Ahh! Fuck!" Her teeth graze over her bottom lip. I am going to have to fuck her. There is going to be no getting around this now.

"Rach, I need to fuck you."

"Fuck me then." She replies breathlessly.

I push her off of my lap and stand her in front of me. She is wearing her little satin dressing gown with a detachable belt.

Oh fuck this is going to be amazing.

I pull the dressing gown off of her and pull the belt though the hoops. Her eyes widen and she gives me a look of pure excitement when she realises what I'm going to do.

"Turn around." I growl at her.

She turns in front me of revealing her beautiful round backside in her soft tiny shorts that show just a peek of the bottom of her glorious cheeks. I grab her hands and pull them around her back. I start to tie the belt around them and I hear Rachel take a sharp intake of breath when I tighten the soft belt around her wrists.

Rachel looks over her shoulder at me.

"Tad?"

Shit is she having second thoughts?

"Yeah baby, too tight?"

She smirks at me and shakes her head.

"Hard Tad. Fuck me so hard."

"Fuck Rach, you're perfect."

I stand abruptly and grab hold of her hair. I pull her head roughly back towards mine and whisper in her ear.

"Promise me you will tell me if it gets too much?"

"Promise." She is panting and desperate, she wants this just as much as I do.

Using my hand in her hair, I roughly turn her around and throw her over my desk. Her breathing is hard and ragged and her arse is swaying from side to side in anticipation. I stand directly behind her and grab hold of her hips to steady her.

"Do not move, do you understand me?"

"Yes." She suddenly stills under my hands.

"Are you wet for me?"

"Fuck yes!" Her voice is full of desperation. God I am going to have so much fun with her. In one swift movement I pull down her tiny shorts to reveal her beautiful rear staring at me. Fuck, her pussy is peeking back at me and is glistening with her excitement. I take two fingers and with no warning at all, push them straight into her.

"Ahhh yes!" She gasps. Her tight slit is soaking wet and clenching hard against my fingers. I start to work her G spot and she starts to cry out. I can see her hands are desperately trying to grab on to something. I move my other hand around the front of her legs and part her beautiful lips so I can find her clit. I gently start to circle my finger around her engorged bud. Her pussy responds by squeezing my fingers even tighter and she lets out little moans with every breath she takes. I start to fuck her with my fingers and rub her clit faster. I feel her hips start to move along with me so I suddenly pull my fingers out and away from her.

"Ahh! What!" She cries out.

"I told you not to move. You moved."

"I'm sorry I won't do it again, I promise."

I walk around the side of her and rub my hand over the soft cheek of her arse. I pull my hand back and with a mild amount of force I spank her sexy little arse.

"Ahh!" She screams out.

I pause briefly and look at her face to check she is ok, she smiles and then wiggles her arse at me!

I pull my hand back again and hit her harder this time, then again on the other cheek. The sound beautifully echoes around my office.

Rachel is panting, eyes closed and biting her bottom lip so hard I think she might make it bleed.

"Are you going to move again?"

"No."

"Do you want me to make you come?"

"Yes! Yes!"

I quickly spank her again.

"Yes what?"

"Ah! Yes please! Please make me come." She cries out desperately.

I drive my fingers back into her greedy pussy and find her clit again with my other hand. I am working both and within seconds I feel her start to shudder around my fingers.

"Ah fuck! Tad! I'm fucking coming!"

I rub her clit even faster and quickly add another finger to fuck her with.

She screams as she comes hard around my fingers. I pound her through her orgasm and her pussy gushes all over my hand.

I quickly pull out my cock and thrust it hard straight into her. She cries out. I can still feel her twitching around my cock from her orgasm. I can't hold back at all. I pound into her with everything I have. I grab her hip with one hand, and her hair in the other so I can pull her back into me. I'm right on the edge already, I pull her hair so she lifts her head from the desk and looks straight ahead.

I plunge my cock in as deep as I can possibly go. The noises that Rach is making are just fucking glorious and are going to tip me over the edge. I scrunch up my eyes and desperately try to calm myself a little. I don't want to come yet, or ever. I want to keep fucking her like this forever.

"Oh Tad! Fuck yes, don't stop!"

"Are you going to come again?" I grunt at her.

"Yes! Yes!"

"Wait for me."

"Fuck Tad, I can't. I'm coming! I'm – AH! Fuck!"

I feel her tighten around my cock and it sends me hurtling over the edge into oblivion. Time feels like it slows down. Rachel's perfect pussy is squeezing every last drop of come from me.

I feel the last of it spurt into her, and I gently fall forwards onto her back.

"How was that?" I ask as I am kissing her neck and shoulders.

"Mmmm... No words..."

I smile to myself.

"That good eh?!"

I stand up and untie her hands, then gently pull out of her. As I do my come spills out of her pussy and starts to trickle down her leg.

So fucking sexy.

"Come on, let's go and have a shower."

I grab her hand and try to pull her up.

"Maybe later. Don't think my legs are working babe."

I laugh.

"You can't stay like that all day!"

I pull her up gently and turn her so she is facing me. Her cheeks are bright red and her eyes have that look of *yeah, I've just been fucked.* She smiles softly at me and it feels like my heart skips a beat and my stomach jumps into my chest. I have no idea what this feeling is, I have never felt anything like it in my life. I pull her close to me.

It's too soon for love you idiot. This is just lust.

Isn't it?

CHAPTER TWENTY EIGHT

A few hours later and we are washed, dressed, and out doing some food shopping. Rach has a doctor's appointment booked for tomorrow morning and is convinced she is fine and apparently is in desperate need of wine, so we've come out to buy a nice bottle. I didn't tell her that I have at least fifty nice bottles of wine in my cellar as I figured we needed to be out and in public so I didn't end up fucking her senseless all day.

We are walking around the shop, just chatting, and I can tell she seems on edge. Maybe she is scared of running into that arsehole husband of hers, or maybe of bumping into anyone she knows and them wondering what she is doing out with me. I look at her and can't help but smile. Her face seems to immediately soften and she grabs my hand in hers. I have genuinely never felt happier in my entire life. I can't ever let this beautiful woman go.

Rachel

S omewhere I can hear a noise. A phone ringing? Beeping? What is that?
It's your alarm idiot, time to wake up.
Oh God that is actually the worst sound in the world.
I roll over in bed and feel around on the bedside table until I feel my phone under my hand. I pick it up and squint at it and can't even work out what I am looking at let alone how to shut the thing up. My brain is still completely asleep and I want to throw

this bloody thing against the wall! I feel a hand snaking around my side and up my arm until it grabs my phone from me and silences it.

"Thanks babe." I murmur. "My brain isn't working yet."

I feel Tad push his body up against mine and he pulls me in close.

"Good morning beautiful."

His voice seems to trickle all the way through me and makes my stomach churn. I just can't believe how I feel about this man, this absolutely wonderful man. I love him, and that both absolutely terrifies me but also makes me feel like I could literally conquer the world. It's unnerving but comforting. And strange, I've never felt like this before, about anyone, yet it feels like the most natural thing, like I've always loved him.

I turn to face him and see his incredible blue eyes staring at me. His perfect smile absolutely melts me.

"How did you sleep?" He gently kisses me on the tip of my nose then looks me straight in the eyes. "Amy more dreams?" His lip curls at one side into a mischievous grin.

"Hmm I don't remember."

It's strange, I always used to remember my dreams, to be honest I found waking up most mornings a real struggle because I wanted to stay dreaming. But now, now I am waking up next to a man who is just incredible, and to be honest it feels more like I am dreaming now.

I lean in to gently kiss him on the lips. I can feel how hard he is already and know I had better get up and dressed before this has a chance to escalate or I will miss my doctor's appointment.

I try to pull away from him to slip out of bed but his grip tightens around me.

"Where are you going?" He groans at me.

"I need to shower you sex pest! I have to leave in about an hour to see the doctor so I can finally have a coffee!"

He nuzzles his face into my neck and starts kissing me.

"We have a whole hour though..." His breath against my neck tickles, he grabs one of the straps of my vest top, pulls it down over my shoulder and starts trailing kisses down my neck across my chest and onto my shoulder. It sends tingles over every part of my body, and more than anything I want to just let him have his wicked way with me, again! But I really do need to get out!

"Tad! Come on! Later, I promise!" I manage to pull myself out of his grip and quickly slide over to the side of the bed out of his reach. He rolls onto his back and growls at me.

He pulls the blanket down revealing his rock hard cock standing, staring at me.

"What am I supposed to do with this?" He mocks a sad face and grabs himself. Jeez I can feel that right down inside me. He is such a bloody tease and he knows it!

"Grab a cold shower after me babe." I grin at him.

He squeezes the tip, and pre come beads out of it.

"Look you've made him cry!"

I can't help but burst out laughing! He laughs too, then throws the blanket back over himself in a pretend strop. I'm still laughing as I walk off into the bathroom.

CHAPTER TWENTY NINE

Tad

Rachel is soaking in a bath so deep that the bubbles are overflowing out of the tub.

"Have I died?" She asks me as I hand her a glass of prosecco.

The doctor said that her blood pressure was almost back to normal. Still slightly high but nothing of any concern. So normal activities can resume, as long as she continues with her medication and doesn't over do things.

I have made sure we've had a very chilled out day today, as I have something special planned for tonight. We have stayed on the sofa for most of the day, and apart from a quick call to check in on Ami and an even quicker call from Robins to check the arsehole husband hasn't been in touch, we've just watched films and Rachel has caught up on all the caffeine she has missed the last couple of days!

We've had a Chinese for dinner, turns out its Rachel's favourite too and we have been using the same take away since it opened.

While she is occupied in the bath, I have been on a hunt around my house for a few things to make tonight more interesting. So far I've found a few candles, some rope, a scarf, ties and some massage oil. I have lit the candles in my bedroom, and set out everything I found on the arm chair. A thought flashes through my head and I quickly sprint back to the kitchen to grab something else.

I can hear Rach finishing up in the bathroom so I take the scarf and go and meet her in there.

I open the door to see her beautiful and naked in front of me. He skin is a rosy pink colour and wet from the slightly too hot water. She has a leg up on the side of the bath, drying it. I can feel my cock coming to life in my trousers already. She catches sight of the scarf in my hand and shoots a curious look at me.

"What that for?"

"I wanted to try something with you."

Her eyes widen and flash with excitement.

"You said you wanted to be controlled, yes?"

She swallows hard and nods her head, her gaze never leaving mine.

"Tied up and spanked too?"

She keeps nodding, her chest rising and falling quickly as her breath speeds up.

"Once we leave this room you will do whatever I tell you to, do you understand?"

She continues to nod.

"I said, do you understand Rachel?"

"Yes. Yes I do."

"And if at any point you get uncomfortable or you're not happy, just say stop, ok?"

She nods again and I widen my eyes at her.

"Sorry, yes, ok."

"Good, now turn around."

Rachel

My heart is thundering in my chest so hard I'm surprised Tad can't see it. I do as I am told and turn slowly around. I feel him walk up behind me. I feel something soft trail up my back and it sends tingles through my entire body. He gets to my neck then wraps a long soft scarf around my head, over my eyes so I can't see anything. Immediately all my senses feel heightened. I can hear his ragged breathing, betraying how excited he is. I can feel the heat from his body and his smooth chest brushing against my back.

He turns me around and leads me by the hands out of the bathroom. Even though I am walking totally blind, I follow him confidently, trusting him completely.

I feel the floor change, from the wooden floorboards in the hallway to the soft carpet in his bedroom. I can smell something sweet, like strawberries maybe? The room is completely silent except from our breathing and shuffling footsteps. Without warning Tad stops, so I stop. I think I am next to his bed but I'm not sure.

I hear Tad walk away, and there is total silence in the room. My skin feels like its tingling all over. I can hear Tad walking towards me. I feel something small and rough trail up my stomach to my chest, it tickles so much my hands instinctively go to cover my chest and I wriggle away from Tad. Suddenly a strong hand grips my wrist, and moves my hand back to my side.

"You don't move unless I tell you too, understand?"

"Yes."

"If you do, you will be punished. Understand?"

I gulp down hard.

"Yes." I say weakly, not though fear but though pure excitement. Every time he speaks, it travels straight down inside of me, and every part of me wants to jump on top of him.

He grabs my chin in his hand and I can feel his breath on my lips.

"You don't do anything without my permission." His free hand trails down my stomach and he cups my sex. "Anything. Understand?"

Oh God. I think I might come just because I know I'm not allowed to yet.

"Yes." I whisper.

"And it's Sir in here." He says at the same time as he roughly thrusts a finger or two into me.

"Yes Sir!" I cry out.

"Good girl."

He lets go of my chin and pulls his fingers out of me, and then puts them straight into my mouth. His fingers are dripping with my salty sweet arousal. I suck his fingers and gently twirl my tongue around them, making little moans as I do. I don't need to see him to know how turned on he is. I can hear every change in his breathing, every little noise he is trying not to make.

He pull his fingers out and fleetingly kisses me on the lips.

He walks around behind me, puts his foot in between mine, the uses it to push my feet out so I am spreading my legs. He then put a hand on my shoulder, and pushes me down.

"Grab each of your ankles." He demands.

I do as I am told. I can feel a slight burn in the back of my legs where they are stretched. I don't care though. My folds are slightly parted in this position, and I am sure that I am dripping down my leg. I have never been this turned on before, and he is barely touching me.

I feel both of his hands on my arse, then I suddenly feel his tongue thrusting inside of me.

Ruthlessly plunging in and out, and licking all around me.

I dig my fingers into my ankles, desperately trying not to move.

Somewhere I hear what sounds like a wrapper being ripped. It sounds a bit like a condom, but I don't know why he would be using one now?

He pulls his tongue away from me and I jump when it is replaced by something cold and hard. He trails it around my soaking wet sex, and it feels smooth. Why does he have a dildo in his house? God I can't think about that now. He is teasing it at my entrance, and I feel like I can hardly breathe.

"Remember, you have to ask for my permission before you come. Ok?"

"Yes sir."

He slowly pushes whatever it is deep inside of me. I throw my head up as I cry out. He suddenly stills.

"Did you just move?"

Shit.

"Sorry Sir."

I put my head back and will myself to stay the fuck still! The way he is talking to me is reminiscent of the way he spoke when he was working in his office yesterday. Totally in control, and ruthless. It is so different from the way Tad normally is, and that in itself is a huge turn on.

He slowly pulls the object out, and back in. It feels cold, and strange, but the way he is pushing it in at the perfect angle is just incredible. He starts to move faster and I can feel my orgasm building up deep inside of me. I try desperately to concentrate on slowing my breathing down.

I feel a hand snake around my hips and I know exactly where it is going. I scrunch up my eyes and try to prepare myself as his fingers find my swollen clit. I moan as he starts to circle my bud, ever so gently, barely touching me at all, but it is enough to make my insides start to clench.

"I need to come!" I cry out.

"That didn't sound much like you asking for permission did it?" He puts slightly more pressure on my clit and starts thrusting the object in and out, faster and faster, I can feel the world start to slip away from beneath me.

"Please! Please can I come?" Oh God it doesn't even matter what answer he gives me because its com- Then he stops. He pulls his hand away from my clit and removes the object and leaves me standing there, panting, right on the edge of release.

I want to turn around and demand he carries on, but instead I just wait there, and hope he carries on.

"Only good girls are allowed to come, and you moved. On your knees!" He barks at me and I immediately drop to my knees. I hear him walk round from behind me. He starts brushing through my hair with his fingers, and then gathers it all in his hand.

"Open."

I open my mouth and he pushes his cock in. I close my mouth around him and hear him try to stifle a groan. He pushes my head, and I take as much of him into my mouth as I can. He holds me there for a few seconds, then he pulls me back. He starts to use my hair to push and pull my head, first slowly, but then speeding up. His hips start to thrust back and forth along with my head. I hope he doesn't get to come.

Abruptly he pulls out of my mouth and pulls me up to standing in front of him.

His hands are squeezing my breasts and then I feel him bite down on my nipple. Oh God this is fucking incredible.

He pushes me backwards and I feel he bed behind my legs.

"Sit down and arms out in front of you."

I do as he says, and then feel something hard and rough around my wrists. It feels like a thick rope. He spends a minute or two tying my wrists together and then he tells me to lay down on the bed. I lay back, and shuffle clumsily until I am as far back as I can get. I hear a loud clicking sound echo round the room and then feel the mattress dip next to me as Tad climbs on.

"Put your hands over your head. And don't move them."

I lift my arms over my head, impressed at how well he has tied the rope. I can't move my wrists apart at all. There is no way I would be able to get out of this by myself. Rather than scaring me, the thought completely turns me on. I am totally at Tad's mercy and it's so hot!

I feel something wet dribble onto my stomach and chest, then I hear that same click again. I can smell a soft sweet smell, and recognise it as baby oil.

Tad's hands start to massage the oil into my skin. He softly rubs the oil into my stomach, then travels up to my breasts. He isn't so gentle with them and he squeezes roughly and runs his finger nails from the tops of my breasts down to my nipples. My breathing is fast and I can hardly concentrate on the whole on moving thing. My back arches up to meet his hands.

"You moved." He mutters accusingly, he sounds firm but like he is smiling. "That's strike one."

Strike one?

Before I can think too much about that his hands are snaking down my body, onto my hips. He trails his fingertips gently across my hip bones, and it takes everything I have not to wiggle under him.

"Open your legs for me." He growls at me.

I open them.

"Mmmm, look at how wet you are for me baby."

He painstakingly trails a finger all the way down from my hip, to my clit, and as he touches it I can't help but whimper. I am so close, I just need him to touch me a little bit more and I can fall away into bliss. He moves his finger away and instead just teases the area around, edging closer and closer to my poor swollen clit, but never really touching it, keeping me just on the edge. My entire body feels like it is on fire, it feels like it is screaming for release. His finger moves further down and starts teasing at my entrance. This is absolute torture. Without even thinking, I thrust my hips up to try to feel his finger inside of me.

"That's strike two."

Shit! Although I wonder what happens when I get to strike three...

He slowly pushes his finger, fingers? I'm not sure, inside of me. Fuck it feels so good. I squeeze tightly around his fingers. He ever so gently starts to massage me from inside and I am scared to breathe in case it tips me over the edge.

"Can I come Sir?" I whisper, desperately trying to hold myself together.

"I'm sorry, I couldn't quite hear that." He is pushing harder and faster inside of me and I feel myself totally fall apart.

"Please can I come?" I cry out, but it doesn't matter, I am coming anyway. There is nothing left in the world except from Tad and his glorious fingers, massaging, and thrusting and making my entire body convulse. I am moving, and coming, and I don't have permission for either, and I am going to be punished, and fuck that just seems to make my orgasm even more intense.

As I feel the waves subside, I still, and wait, in silence. He doesn't say anything. He pulled his fingers out of me at some point and I didn't even notice. I'm not even sure he is still on the bed with me.

"That was strike three, four, and five!"

Five strikes?!

"Roll over onto your stomach and put your arse in the air."

I'm absolutely drained after my orgasm, and that with the combination of being tied up means I probably do the least sexy roll of my life. I get slightly onto my knees, and I feel him next to me, he pushes a pillow under my hips.

"You can lay down now."

I lay down, and wait.

"I told you that if you disobeyed me you would be punished didn't I?"

Suddenly I am wide awake, fear and excitement course through me as I think I realise what he meant by strikes.

"Five strikes Rachel, and you are going to count after every one, do you understand?"

Fuck, I'm scared.

I know he won't *hurt* me, but this still might hurt.

"Yes Sir." It's barely a whisper.

I feel his hand on my bum cheek, he is stroking it, and teasing his fingertips over it. He lifts his hand off, and the anticipation is intense. Suddenly he slaps me hard, right in the middle of my cheek, the sound of it cuts through the silence in the room. I gasp loudly. It stings, but it doesn't hurt, in fact, the feeling of the pillow on my swollen clit and the warmth radiating from my arse, feels fucking incredible.

"One." I whisper. I feel his hand slide into my own and he gives me a gentle squeeze. This is why I love this man, even in the middle of this completely intense situation he's checking I'm ok. I squeeze it back and smile, hoping he is looking at my face.

Suddenly he hits my other cheek with slightly more force.

"Ahh! Two!"

Quickly he hits me again.

"Three!!"

And again.

"Ahhh Four!" I yell out. Fuck that one hurt, but it's the most intense, amazing type of pain.

He teases his fingers over my sore, hot cheeks, with the very tips of his fingers, and the sensation makes me cry out. It tingles, and sends electricity through me, to every part of my body.

I can feel the adrenaline rushing through me as I wait for the final blow.

When it comes, it's in exactly the same spot as the last one. It burns this time, and I am pleased that it's the last one.

"Five!" I pant. My breathing is ragged and I am feeling so horny. I need him to fuck me into oblivion.

He gently stokes my backside, and I wiggle around under him. The sensation is so intense, the tingling sends shivers up my whole body.

I feel him stand up off of the bed, and he walks around to the side where my arms are hanging off. After a minute or two of untying the rope, my hands are free. They tingle as a rush of blood comes back to them. Tad then lifts me up so I am on my knees on the bed facing him, and he pulls off my blindfold. His eyes look intense, his lips are parted, and he looks just as turned on as me. I can't help it. I throw myself into him and kiss him like I need him as much as I need oxygen. I have never felt so close to anyone before. I feel tears pricking at my eyes, not because of what just happened, but because I can't believe how lucky I have been, that I get to be here with this man. Our hands are frantically searching each other's bodies, and I reach down to find Tad's ridiculously hard cock. He moans into my mouth as I grab it, then he throws me backwards onto the bed. He climbs on top of me, lifts my legs over his shoulders and thrusts into me all in one quick move. He fills me up completely and it feels amazing. He quickly and roughly pounds into me, harder and faster. I can feel my orgasm building again. He moves his thumb to my clit and starts massaging it, edging me closer and closer.

"Come with me baby!" He cries out. And that is all it takes.

Time has passed. I have absolutely no idea how much time. We both practically passed out on each other after we came. I stroke my hand up Tad's back and he kisses my neck and rolls off of me. I sit up and mentally prepare myself for the journey from the bed to the bathroom to clean myself up. Then out the corner of my eye I see something that makes me stop dead in my tracks.

"What the...?!"

Tad lifts his head slightly.

"What's wrong?" He asks sleepily.

"Tad, why the fuck is there a carrot with a condom on it on the floor?!"

He used a carrot to fuck me?!

I have absolutely no words.

"Uh... Improvisation?" I turn to look at him and he is grinning at me. His grin is infectious and I can't help but start laughing.

"What the fuck Tad!" I grab the nearest pillow and playfully hit him around the head with it. "I think we might need to invest in some real sex toys!"

He pulls me into his arms on the bed and kisses me while we are both laughing.

CHAPTER THIRTY

Tad

"You wake me up at six am just to tell me the contracts are through? Could that not have waited till slightly later in the day?"

"Tad, normally you're up at five! I'm worried about you. You normally check in with me every day. I know you've left Scott to deal with things this week but I'm worried about you. You haven't answered any of my calls or e-mails. What's been going on?" Suze sounds worried. I really shouldn't have left her in the dark completely.

"Yeah. I'm sorry Suze, things have been..." I scratch my head as I try to think of the right word to describe the last few days. "Crazy. I just need some time. I'll be back first thing Monday, don't panic. And I've been in touch with Scott and listening in to conference calls and he's doing great without me. You don't give him enough credit you know."

"Yeah yeah, Scott is great, I know that. I'm more worried about you!"

"Well don't be worried! I'm fine. I'm better than fine. In fact, I am better than I have been in a really, *really* long time." I smile as I think about the beautiful woman naked and asleep in my bed upstairs.

Suze stays silent on the phone.

"Scouts honour." I joke.

"Hmm... Well ok. You're going to have to have a look over those contracts this morning though, can you manage that?"

"Yes, of course I can, e-mail them over and I'll make a coffee and take a look, ok?"

"Already sent Tad. Call me later ok? You sound strange..."

"Talk to you later Suze, love ya!"

"Yes, I'm sure you do..."

I smile to myself as I put my phone down on the kitchen counter. I sound *strange* because I am happy. I haven't been happy in a long time. Even before Seb...

I feel arms snaking around my waist and I jump as I realise that Rach must have crept down the stairs.

"Who is Suze eh? Do I have anything to worry about?" She says through a smile as she is nibbling at my neck from behind.

I turn around and pull her in close for a kiss.

"Susan is my personal assistant. And a saint for putting up with me as her boss!"

"Is she the really little lady from the fundraiser? With the little red specs?"

"Yep, that's Suze. She is going to love you." Rachel's cheeks flush red, and she smiles at me.

"I've got coffee brewing gorgeous."

Her eyes widen in excitement. She almost looks as excited as last night, almost!

I walk over to the coffee and pour us both a mug, I add a bit of milk and one sugar and take it over to Rachel, who is practically drooling!

She takes a sip and moans into her coffee. I just stare at her, smiling to myself.

She lowers the cup and catches me staring at her. I quickly turn to my cup of coffee.

"Your coffee is almost as good as your fucking." She grins at me from behind her mug.

"What do you fancy for breakfast beautiful? I mean, you know my cooking skills are limited so I can only really offer you toast or cereal."

"Actually Celine has text, she's got the day off and she wants to meet early for breakfast. Although if I'm honest, I think she just wants to hear all the gossip!"

"Will my ears be burning later then?"

"Probably." She smiles and takes a long sip of coffee. "I'm gonna go up and have a shower and then head straight out. If that's ok?"

I walk over to her and hold her chin in my hand.

"Babe, you don't have to ask permission, not now anyway." I wink at her and she giggles.

She walks off towards the stairs and pulls off the shirt she had on.

She is gloriously naked underneath, and I want to jump her, right there on the stairs.

"You just gonna stand gawking or you gonna come help me in the shower?" She says as she starts walking up the stairs.

I won't admit it to her, but I definitely ran out of the kitchen and up the stairs to catch up with her.

Rachel

Celine is just staring at me. Eyes and mouth wide open.

"Cel, stop it! The wind will change and you'll be stuck that way!" I giggle.

I have just finished telling Celine all the details of the last three days.

All the details.

I mockingly wave my hand in front of her eyes.

"Hello, anyone in there?!"

She blinks and looks at me and a huge smile crosses her face.

"You absolute fucking minx!"

We both burst out laughing.

I take a long sip of my coffee and wait for her to say something.

"Like, he actually spanked you? Like hit you, hit you?" She leans in and whispers.

I just nod.

"And you liked it?" She seems genuinely confused.

I over exaggerate my nod.

"Not gonna lie Rach, I don't get it. You spend years with an arsehole husband who on more than one occasion has hit you, and now you are actively asking a nice man to hit you?"

"God Cel, it's nothing like that! With Kevin, he hit me because he was an absolute scum bag. There are no words to describe what Kevin is-"

"Yes there are, cunt."

"Um yeah ok, that word then. But he wanted to control me, because he was, that word. He didn't ever love me, or do anything for me, and he hit me out of hate and aggression. With Tad, I don't know. It's so hard to explain. We have the most amazing sex, like it's the sex I have always dreamt of and never thought I'd have! He knows exactly what I want even without me having to ask. He takes control, literally, when I'm tied up I don't have to worry about anything. I know he is going to look after me in every way. And everything he does, he does it for me. And even though I'm the one tied up, I know I am in totally control at any time. All I have to do is say stop, and he will stop."

"But how do you know that?"

"How did you know that you were going to spend the rest of your life with Dan after a few hours of knowing him?"

"Ok, good point, well played."

"Like I said it's hard to explain. I just know that he will never ever really *hurt* me. And it's the hottest thing I've ever *ever* done in my life!"

"And you're happy?" Her face softens and I beam at her.

"So happy. With Tad anyway, I mean the rest of my life is totally up the shitter, but at least there is one part of my life that is incredible."

"Yeah, I take it there's been no word from Kevin?"

"Nope. And Ami is home on Friday so I'm going to have to bite the bullet and explain to her why she won't be going home. I haven't technically asked my parents, but I'm hoping they will put us both up until I can sort out some money to find a place." I bury my face in my hands. "God this is a nightmare Cel. I haven't even braved the news or any newspapers because I am totally dreading what is being said about Kevin. Not because of him, obviously, but everyone knows us around here, all the kids know who Ami's dad is. I don't want this to affect her."

Celine grabs my hand from across the table.

"She is a strong kid Rach, I know this is going to be hard from her, but she will get through it. You both will. And I am always going to be here for you both, you know that don't you?"

I smile and nod at her. I know she is right. Ami is a truly amazing child, and so grown up for her age. Which is why I have to tell her sooner rather than later. She will be hurt that I have kept this from her.

"So, how bad is it?" I ask Celine.

"How bad is what?"

"The press. What they're saying about Kevin."

Her face falls and I know it's not good. Although I didn't expect it to be.

"Yeah, it's not great babe. Of course the official release is just that police need to speak to him in regards to a suspicious death. But the tabloids have gone and interviewed supposed friends and whoever, and concocted their own little story. Which to be honest sweets, it's pretty much what the police suspect anyway." I guess it's not a massive jump for the press, especially if people are talking to them... "They've managed to get hold of photos of him and that woman. And also a few other women, but they've not been named and their faces are blurred in the photos."

Other women?

God this is all too much to take in. I think Cel can read my face so she stops and takes a long sip of her coffee.

"I did see something that might make you smile whilst looking through the papers this morning though." I look up at her and she has a playful smile on her face.

"What was it?"

"Hang on!" She jumps out of her seat and heads towards the little table at the front of the shop where all of the days newspapers are kept. She has a quick look through and walks back over with one of those tabloid papers that I hope most people only buy to line their cat litter boxes instead of actually reading!

As she is flicking through the pages, I see a brief glimpse of Kevin on one of the pages, and I feel sick in the pit of my stomach. But before I really have time to think about it, Celine is thrusting a photo of me and Tad into my face.

What?!

It was taken when we went shopping on Monday, it's of me on tiptoes kissing him on the cheek, there's a second smaller photo of us looking lovingly in each other's eyes holding hands. The headline reads ***Looks like love!***

I look up at Celine, totally mortified, but she is beaming from ear to ear.

"Why are you smiling?" I ask her, snatching the paper from her so I can read what has been written.

"Why aren't you? Look at how happy you both look, it's cute!"

Looks like love is finally on the cards for one of the UK's most eligible and desirable millionaires. Thaddeus Turner, 33, CEO of Turner and Prescott Holdings has always shunned questions in interviews when asked about women and he never attends events with anyone. But it seems after the recent heartbreak of losing his younger brother just a few weeks ago, he has finally found someone to help heal his heart.

"Uh I can't read this shit." I throw he paper on the table. "Does it say my name?"

"No babe, no name."

It's a pretty clear picture of my face though, as far as everyone else knew up until a few days ago I was happily married. Now my son of a bitch husband is on page three of the tabloids, being accused of murdering one of the women he has been sleeping with behind my back, and I'm lurking around the back pages kissing a millionaire in the fucking Co-Op.

"Hey!" Celine grabs my hand again. "You don't need to be worrying about what anyone else thinks. Everyone else will know now what that cunt has put you through for the last nine years, and they will be happy you're happy. The important people anyway. Anyone else, fuck them!"

I manage to crack a smile, I know she is right.

"I'd better get a move on babe, I need to call Ami. I mean, I'm not sure she often reads the papers but if anyone else told her any of this before me she would never forgive me."

"Why don't you come back to mine and we can call her together?"

I smile at her, she really is the most wonderful friend I could ever ask for.

CHAPTER THIRTY ONE

'm sat on the sofa at Cel's house and I'm waiting for my Mum to answer the phone. I'd better check in with her as no doubt she is worrying after what Dad will have told her.

"Hey Mummy bear."

"Oh Rachel darling, I've been so worried about you. Your father told me everything that happened then made me promise not to call you to give you some space to get your head around things. Your bloody father. I'm so sorry. How are you?"

"I'm actually ok Mum, I promise."

"Hmmm." She isn't convinced. This must all be a hell of a lot for her to take in.

"Listen Mum, I was wondering if it would be ok for me and Ami to stay with you for a little while, just until I can sort somewhere to live. I can't go back to that house, but I have no access to any money at the moment."

"Rachel, you didn't need to ask, of course you can."

"Thanks Mum."

"I'm worried about you Rachel. Have you heard anything from Kevin?"

"No, nothing. And neither have the police." I pause for a moment and breathe out heavily. "Mum, I need to tell Ami. Not everything, not now, but she will be so upset I have kept this from her."

"She isn't a stupid girl, she knows something is going on. She is just coming now, I'll put her on."

"Ok, thanks mum, love you."

"Love you to darling."

Celine is sitting beside me and she grabs hold of my other hand while I wait for Ami to take the phone.

"Mummy!!"

"Hey baby, how are you?"

"I'm amazing, I'm having so much fun."

"That's good honey, you missing me?"

"Yeah, I bought you a present! I love it here, but I can't wait to go home and see you."

I close my eyes and take a deep breath in.

"Listen baby, I have to tell you something. When you get back on Friday we are going to stay with Nanny and Gramps for a little while."

"Why?"

"Well, uh, Daddy has got himself in a little bit of trouble, and I just think it's best we don't stay in our house for a while."

I look at Celine, and she gives me a little smile and nod.

"Are you and Dad getting a divorce?" She asks matter of factly.

"I don't want to lie to you honey, and I know this is going to be hard to hear, but yes, me and your dad aren't together anymore, and we will be getting a divorce."

"Ok."

"Ok...? You aren't upset?"

"Mummy, I know that you and Daddy don't love each other and I know Daddy doesn't make you happy. The same thing happened with Louise's parents and they got a divorce. I get it. It's fine."

This kid will never cease to amaze me.

"Well I'm glad you're so understanding baby."

"Mum, what did you mean by Dad is in trouble?"

"Look, it's a bit difficult to explain, but your Dad has done something wrong..." I don't know what to tell her. I don't want to tell her everything. She is nine years old! She shouldn't have to deal with any of this. But at the same time, this will be out there and I can't risk someone else telling her. "I promise I will explain everything to you on Friday sweety. But you don't need to worry about anything, ok?"

"Ok Mummy. But are you ok?"

"I'm great baby. Are you ok?"

"I'm ok." In the background I can hear a load of kids shouting.

"They your friends baby?"

"Yeah, the swimming pool has got an inflatable assault course going up, so we are all going to go. Grandad is going to come too." She laughs down the phone. This doesn't seem to have phased her at all...

"Well you make sure you get some photos of grandad making a fool out of himself!"

She laughs again.

"Pass me over to him quickly ok?"

"Ok Mummy, I love you!"

"She seems fine?" I mouth to Celine.

"Hey princess."

"Hey Daddy, listen I've just said to Ami that basically me and Kevin are getting a divorce and he is in a bit of trouble, but that's it. I want to tell her the rest in person, so just if she asks- ok?"

"Yeah, ok sweetie."

"Just keep a close eye on her, she seemed ok on the phone..."

"Don't worry, I will."

"Oh, and Dad. Please, please don't scare her new friends off with your tiny red speedos!"

"Hey, I still look good in a speedo!"

"Gross! Love you Dad."

"Love you to princess."

That seemed far too easy. I hope she is actually ok, and not hiding it for my sake.

"I told you. Kids are resilient. And she is a super smart kid." Celine leans in and hugs me.

"Is it too early for wine?" I am only half joking.

Celine checks her phone.

"11.43 on a Wednesday morning. Bah, it's nearly lunch time. I'll grab a bottle!"

I lean back into the sofa and close my eyes.

This has by far been the craziest week of my entire life.

I feel the sofa dip next to me and open my eyes to see Celine sitting next to me holding a bottle of rosé and two wine glasses.

"This is why you are my best friend!" I laugh as I sit up and grab a glass.

I hear a buzzing noise, and it is my phone telling me I have a text. I see Tad's name light up and my stomach starts fluttering.

Don't hurry back, but I miss you xx

Celine is reading too and squeals loudly.

"Oh my God Rach!!"

"What?" I say through the biggest grin.

"He loooves you!" She sings at me.

"No he does not!"

"He loooves you, oh yes he loooves you!"

"Shut up!" I grab a pillow and jokingly hit her with it.

"So what is going on with you two then. I mean apart from all the amazing kinky sex?"

"Well, I said to him if he wanted to keep things casual because of my insane amounts of drama then that was fine by me, although at this point I really don't think it would be. But he said he couldn't do casual with me, and wanted to give this a real go." I look over at Celine and she is smiling with her mouth wide open.

"Woah." She finally says and then pours us both a glass of wine.

She picks hers up and proposes a toast.

"Congratulations on bagging Mr. Millionaire!" She laughs.

CHAPTER THIRTY TWO

Tad

It's only been a few hours. How do I miss her already? This is ridiculous, this time last week I didn't even know she existed, and now I am sat twiddling my thumbs waiting for her to come home. I've looked through all the Serenity contracts and amended parts and sent it back to Scott to get it all signed off. There is absolute shit on the TV and social media is just winding me up. I've run upstairs to get changed into some shorts and a t-shirt, I have a small gym set up in my cellar that I don't think I have ever really used. I normally prefer to go out, but I don't want to be out when Rach gets back, so I'll go and blow off some steam down there instead.

I'm just finishing off on the treadmill when I hear my doorbell go.

I should give her a key.

It's a bit too soon for a key though isn't it?

After what you did to her yesterday? Nothing is too soon!

My heart is pounding in my chest, I want to say it's because of the weights I have just lifted and the run up the stairs to answer the door, but in reality it's definitely because I am so excited to open the door and see my beautiful girl.

I'm dripping with sweat and I quickly pull my shirt off over my head as I walk towards the front door so she gets an eyeful when I open it.

As I open the door I give her my most intense *come fuck me stare*. Only to find it's not her, but Scott.

Fuck.

"Jesus Tad!"

"Scott, what are you doing here?"

"I need the contracts signed dude, figured I'd drop them round in person seeing as I haven't seen you in ages. Wanted to check in on you." He looks me up and down with his brow furrowed.

I quickly walk into my front room, grab a top from my sofa and throw it on.

"Expecting company were we?" He is smirking at me.

I really don't feel like telling him about this right now.

"No, just been working out."

He shoots me a look across the room.

"Right, so you just open the door shirtless and sweaty, biting your lip for everyone do you?"

"I was not biting my lip!"

"You might as well have been!"

I walk into my kitchen to grab a bottle of water from my fridge.

"Want one?"

"No..." Scott looks bewildered.

"What?"

"You're different..."

"No I'm not!"

"Hmm... So when are you coming back to work?"

"I'll be back in the office Monday. Where are those contracts?"

I want him out of here before Rach gets back, I don't want the third degree now, and I know exactly what he will think. What I assume most people would think if their best friend had all but moved in a woman who he hadn't even known a week, who also happened to be married to a psychotic murderer.

"They're here. Trying to get rid of me?"

"No, just need a shower that's all."

"Go up and shower, I'll make coffee, then we can go over the contracts and you can triple check and sign."

Fuck sake! Just go away!

After the fastest shower of my life, I've just finished wrapping a towel around my waist when I hear the doorbell.

Bollocks.

I run down the stairs so I can open the door before Scott. I open the door and Rach is standing there, her beautiful brown hair all windswept from the sea breeze. She looks me up and down and before I have the chance to say anything she grabs my shoulders and pulls me in for a kiss. I'm trying to stop her so I can tell her that we have company, but my God, when this woman touches me it's like I have no control over my body anymore. My hands absentmindedly travel to her beautiful arse and she moans slightly into my mouth. I feel that noise deep inside of me and for a second I totally forget where I am.

Until I hear Scott clearing his throat and I'm brought sharply back down to earth. We quickly pull apart and both look over to Scott, who is standing with his mouth wide open.

Fuck fuck fuck!

"Um, Scott, this is Rachel. Rachel, this is Scott, my business partner."

Rachel's cheeks are bright red as she walks over to Scott to shake his hand.

"Hi, nice to meet you." She says meekly. "Sorry Tad, I didn't realise you had company. I'll just go and make some coffee."

"No need." Scott says, "I just made a pot, I'll pour you a mug while Romeo over there gets dressed."

She giggles and they both walk into the kitchen together.

Scott shoots me a look as if to say *what the fuck?*

I run upstairs, open my drawers and throw on the first things I find, then run back downstairs. They are still in the kitchen when I get down. Scott is telling Rachel about how he met me when I was in junior school.

"I taught him how to stand up for himself. There was this group of bigger boys who always picked on him because of who his dad was, half their dads were locked up, and the other half were well on their way to joining them. Anyway, I taught Tad how to punch properly. And from then our friendship blossomed."

They both laugh. As I walk into the kitchen Scott shoots me that look again.

Rachel stands with her coffee.

"I'll leave you two to it." She kisses me on the cheek and walks out.

Scott is just staring at me waiting to talk.

"Ok, so I met someone." I say after a few moments of uncomfortable silence.

"Yeah, I see that! How long has this been going on? How come you didn't tell me man, I thought we were friends!"

I run my hands through my damp hair.

"To be honest I haven't known her all that long, she's been in a bit of trouble which is why I needed this week off."

I give in and tell him everything, well not everything, but all the important bits. I don't think Scott needs to hear about all our bedroom antics.

"So, let me just get this straight." Scott whispers. "You met this woman less than a week ago, her husband, *husband!* You know, the guy she is *married* to, has murdered someone, and now you two are shacked up and in love and are going to live happily ever after?"

"I didn't say we were in love, and we aren't shacked up. I'm just looking after her until her parents get back so she can go and stay with them."

Scott just stares at me.

"I know! Alright! I know this is crazy! But, fuck man, I've never felt like this before. Ever. I'm happy. *She* makes me happy. And I know this is new, and complicated. So fucking complicated, and yes I probably shouldn't be getting involved. But I can't stay away."

"Jesus Tad! Just be careful, please."

After what feels like hours of going through the contracts, they are finally all signed and Scott has a meeting set up Friday with Harris for him to sign and finalise it all.

There is a knock on my office door.

"Yeah babe." I call out to Rach.

"Sorry, hope I'm not disturbing. I'm making more coffee, do either of you want any?"

"We're all good thanks, Scott is leaving now anyway." I answer her. She smiles at me, and fuck it melts me, and she walks off.

"Fuck man." Scott says from somewhere in the distance.

"What?"

"You've got it bad!" He laughs.

Scott has just left, and I find Rachel busy in the kitchen cooking. I just stand at the door watching her cutting some chicken, and then stirring one pan, then going to another, and back to the chicken.

"You just gonna stand there watching or you gonna come and help me?"

I walk over to her and stand behind her. I gently kiss her on the side of the neck and let my hands snake down her sides. She wiggles under me.

"Hey, sharp knife! I like having all my fingers you know!" She laughs at me.

"And this is why I shouldn't even be allowed in a kitchen, never mind allowed to cook. What you making?"

"I fancied a chicken pie, is that ok?"

"Sounds delicious."

I just watch her cook for a while. She is frying off onions and mushrooms in one pan and making a white sauce in another, once the chicken is in and all cooked, he mixes everything together and puts it in a bowl to one side.

"How was your morning with Celine?"

"It was great thank you. I spoke to Ami."

"Oh yeah?"

"Yeah. Told her me and Kevin are getting divorced, that we would be staying with my parents for a while and that Daddy was in a bit of trouble..."

"Fuck. That must have been a lot for her to take in. Is she ok?"

"That's wat I thought, but as it turns out, she said she knew I didn't love him, and he didn't make me happy, and her friend's parents got a divorce, and its *fine*."

"Woah." This kid sounds like a tough cookie. "What did she say about him being in trouble?"

"She didn't really focus on that bit, and I didn't want to overwhelm her. I'll explain it all to her Friday."

"You're a wonderful mum Rachel." I smile at her. She blushes.

"I'm far from it. But that girl is my absolute world, and I would do anything for her."

I go back to watching her effortlessly gliding around the kitchen.

"So I saw something interesting in the paper today." She says.

"What was that?"

"Bloody photos of us when we went shopping the other day. Apparently according to the daily pile of rubbish, you have finally found love."

Oh bloody hell. Fucking newspapers and their reporters. Reaching for any story about my love life they can find.

"It's amazing. I have done so much for so many companies over the years, donated millions to charities, yet all the papers seem to care about is if I've got a girlfriend yet!"

"Don't you just love the press!" She laughs but I can tell she is uncomfortable.

"Hey, you ok?"

"Yeah, it's just odd you now. Kevin is splashed all over the papers as a cheating murderer, and then lurking around in the back pages I'm there kissing you holding your hand. People are going to be gossiping all over. And its only time before the papers get wind that I am who I am."

I walk up to her, turn her around and wrap my arms around her.

"Fuck what everyone else thinks."

"That's what Cel said."

"That's because she's smart."

I kiss her softly on the top of her head and let her get back to rolling out some pastry.

I hear her phone buzzing from next to her on the counter.

"My dad has text, can you read it for me please babe?" She wiggles her doughy fingers at me as I reach over to get her phone.

I read out loud.

"Hey princess. I have transferred some money into your bank account. It's a gift so please don't worry about paying me back. Use it to buy some bits for the spare rooms at our house to make it more homely for you both. And buy yourself something nice with anything left over. Ami is having a great time. Love you lots"

I look up at Rachel and she looks slightly annoyed.

"Bloody hell." She mutters under her breath as she goes to wash her hands.

I hand her phone back to her, and she quickly logs into her online banking.

"£1000! What the bloody hell does he want me to buy with that?"

I guess she will actually be going to live with her parents when they get back then. My heart drops a little. I knew that. But I guess I had hoped she would just stay here.

And what about her kid?

Fuck. This is so complicated.

She is furiously typing a message back to her Dad. When she is finished she puts her phone down and takes a deep breath in and out.

"You ok?" I ask.

"Yeah, I just hate being treated like a charity case!"

"I don't think that's what this is! I think your dad is trying to help you out because he loves you." Her face softens.

"Yeah, I know that really."

"I take it you're close to your parents then?" I ask her.

"Yeah, so close. They are amazing. And they are absolutely incredible with Ami. Are you close with your mum?"

"Yeah, not really. My Dad and I were super close, but my Mum was always quite distant really."

She comes over and leans her head into my shoulder.

Her phone starts vibrating again, probably her dad. We both look at the screen to see an incoming call from a withheld number.

My heart starts pounding, and I can hear her breathing quicken and she looks terrified.

"Answer on speaker phone." I say.

She presses the speaker phone button and answers.

"H-Hello?"

"You fucking whore."

I feel my blood run cold and I see the colour completely drain from Rachel's face.

In a second I have my phone out and I am recording the conversation. I leave my phone in the kitchen and run to get my landline to phone Robins.

"Kevin. The police are looking for you, you should"-

"I know they are looking for me, thanks to you and your big fucking mouth. But they won't be able to find me."

Robins' number is ringing out, and I am silently willing him to answer his fucking phone. After what feels like an age he answers and before he has the chance to say a word I butt in.

"Kevin Blackford is on the phone to Rachel."

I give him my address and he says someone will be there in a couple of minutes.

I go back and Rachel looks terrified.

"I saw you with that cunt in the paper. You fucking slag. How long have you been fucking him then?"

153

"Kevin I don't want to speak to you, you should call the police and"-

"Fuck you Rachel. I'm going to kill you, do you hear me. I tried to give you everything and you threw it in my fucking face at every turn. Now you've ruined my life, and you think you get to just ride off into the sunset with someone else? That's not how it fucking works. Until death do we part Rachel. And I'm going to fucking kill you."

The line goes dead and Rachel just stares blankly at her phone.

I pull her into my arms and we just stand in silence for a while.

The doorbell and a loud banging on the door interrupts us, and I open it to find two officers standing at the door. I recognize the young woman as the one who helped Celine get Rachel's clothes at her house.

"Hi, Detective Robins is on his way but he told us to come first. We understand Mr. Blackford made contact?"

"Uh, yeah. He called Rachel. She's in the kitchen. Please, come in."

I show them through to the kitchen where I find Rachel standing in exactly the same spot I left her in. I go back and wrap my arms around her.

"Mrs. Blackford?" The young officer asks.

I feel Rachel cringe under my arms.

"*Please* don't call me that. It's Rachel."

"Sorry, Rachel. Are you able to tell me what he said?"

"Uh, well he said that he saw a photo of me and Tad in the paper, and then he said something about till death do us part, and then said he was going to kill me." Her voice is monotone and completely void of any emotion. I can't tell if she is trying to keep it together, or if she's just in shock.

The officer from her house, Lucy? I think, is jotting down what Rachel has said in a little note pad.

"I don't suppose he gave away any clues as to where he was?"

Rachel looks at me.

"I don't really know. I can't remember, I don't think so."

"He said that you wouldn't be able to find him. I recorded the conversation on my phone." I say to the officers.

"That's great, when Robins gets here I will get him to check it out."

There is a tap at my front door and the other officer goes to open it.

CHAPTER THIRTY THREE

Rachel

After what feels like hours of questions and waiting around for another call, the police have all finally left. Robins has left two police officers at Tad's house tonight to keep watch, just in case Kevin calls again. Or turns up. I can't even think about the latter.

Tad has also been on the phone to his own personal security, and has a few guards coming to keep an eye on the house.

I'm sat on the sofa with an untouched glass of wine that Tad has poured me. I don't even think wine will make me feel better right now.

I was on such a high this morning. And then of course Kevin comes and ruins it all.

I hear footsteps behind me and then Tad's strong arms wrap around my shoulders, giving me a hug from behind the sofa.

"Can I get you anything?"

I just shake my head.

God, he doesn't need all of this. He could have any woman in the world, and he manages to choose the one who is married to a crazy psycho murderer.

He comes to sit next to me.

"Rach?"

I turn to look at him. He is looking at me so intensely, like he knows exactly what I am thinking.

"He's not going to lay a finger on you, you know that right?"

He takes his hand and strokes down my cheek before cupping my chin in his hand. He leans in close.

"I won't let him get anywhere near you, ever again. I promise." He says it with such strength that part of me believes him.

"This isn't just some random person making a threat though. This is someone who has already killed someone. He knows he has lost everything now, me, his daughter, his life! He has nothing left to lose, and that is when someone is most dangerous."

"Rachel, he is angry. He is not thinking with his head, but with his heart, and that is when people make the most mistakes. He didn't come up with some master plan to kill that poor girl. It was in the heat of the moment. He isn't clever enough to be able to get to you without someone getting wind of him coming. You're being watched now by the police, and by my guards. He may come for you, and if he does he will be caught. The police are still looking for him, I have men looking for him and he is bound to mess up somewhere. He will be caught long before he manages to get anywhere near you, I swear it Rachel."

I believe him. I believe every word that has come out of his mouth. I just trust this man with everything I have and I trust that he will look after me and keep me safe. I can already feel some of the knots in my stomach melting away.

Tad smiles at me and it's like my world has been put back together. It just feels like no matter what happens to me anymore, none of it matters because I have him. And I never ever want to lose him.

"I love you Tad."

WHAT?!

Oh my God! The words came out of my mouth before I had any idea I was even thinking them. My eyes are wide and I have clenched my lips shut tightly.

I stare at Tad for something. His face is totally unreadable, and that completely throws me. I can normally get some sense of what is going through his mind when I look at him. But his face just looks blank.

I can't believe you said that you idiot! Quick do something before he asks you to leave.

He takes a deep breath in.

"Rachel I"–

But before he has a chance to say anything I throw myself at him. My lips are all over his. At first it feels like he is trying to hold back, but then he puts an arm around me and lifts me effortlessly onto his lap. He slows down my frantic kissing. He ever so gently finds my tongue with his and slowly twirls it around mine, before pulling back and sucking gently on my bottom lip. He wraps my legs around his waist, stands up and starts to carry me up the stairs, all with his lips never leaving mine.

When we get up to his room, he gently places me on his bed and stands up so he can take off my shirt. I lift my arms to help him pull it off over my head. Once he has thrown it across the room he takes off his own and throws it too. He gets on the bed and pulls me next to him as he starts to kiss me again. It's so intense, so passionate. He starts to lay down and I follow him. He starts fumbling around with the button on my jeans and pulls them down as soon as he undoes it. I kick my jeans off while he is taking off his own.

I roll onto my back and he lays on top of me. I can feel his cock, hard and ready, in between my legs. I trail my hands all over his back and neck, and feel the goosebumps over his skin. He stops kissing me, and just looks at me. He brushes my hair behind my ears.

Fuck. He's going to say it too. Is he?

"You are so beautiful."

Oh.

I lean in to kiss him once again to hide my hurt. It's insane. It's far too soon for me to love him, definitely too soon to have said it. I'm lucky he hasn't kicked me out of the front door, I shouldn't be expecting him to say it back.

I feel him pulling my knickers down, I lift my hips so he can slide them off. He starts to pull his boxers down and he stops kissing me again. He looks me straight in the eyes as he ever so slowly and gently pushes his solid length into me. I want to throw my head back and close my eyes, but I can't move my eyes from his. I gasp softly as he fills me up entirely.

I manage to look away and I turn my head slightly. Tad lowers his face to my neck and gently starts kissing and nibbling my exposed skin. He starts to slowly thrust in and out. Painfully slowly, filling up every inch of me. It feels so good. Too good. This isn't just sex, or kinky fucking. This is making love, and my god that phrase has always made me want to vomit a little. But only because I didn't understand it. I get it now. Completely.

I look back in his eyes and he stills for a few seconds. And for those few seconds there is absolutely nothing else in the world. Just me and Tad, joined together, him filling me completely. It's all too much for me. This man has made me feel things I never ever thought possible and I don't know how to deal with them. I have to look away from his eyes. I am already in so deep, so much deeper than him. I wrap my arms around his neck and pull him back in to kiss me. He starts moving his hips again, slightly faster this time. I kiss him harder and then trail my hands down his back so I can grab his beautiful tight arse. I push him deeper into me with every thrust. He is hitting me in just the right spot, his pubic bone is rubbing on my clit. I will never ever get tired of this feeling. Tad must know I am close and he starts to pound me harder. He stops kissing me and pulls his face up so he can look at me again.

I can feel my orgasm building in every part of me, I start to clench tightly around Tad and then feel reality slip away from me for a moment.

"Aah God Tad!" My hips buck up to meet his and I feel him slow his thrusts as he explodes inside of me.

"Aaah Rachel!"

He finishes and falls onto my chest. We both lay there and steady our breathing in silence. Tad is tracing his fingers along my stomach, and I am running my fingers through his hair.

CHAPTER THIRTY FOUR

I'm running. Or at least I am trying to run. But I just can't seem to go any faster than a jog. I know I can run faster than this. I will my feet to move.

Come on! He is coming!

"Rachel?"

Fuck. I can't let him catch me. Please legs, run!

"RACHEL!"

My legs are useless so I hide behind a tree instead. There are hundreds of trees, small trees, tall trees that reach the sky and have huge, wide trunks, yet I hide behind the one that barely covers even one of my legs. I am looking around to see if I can see him but suddenly a thick fog creeps in and I can't see anything at all.

I turn around and there he is, standing right above me holding a knife.

"Till death do us part dear wife."

He lunges forwards at me and I scream.

I sit bolt upright, awoken suddenly from my nightmare. I am breathing heavily and covered in sweat. Tad is next to me, still asleep. It takes a while to steady myself and realise where I am and that I am safe. I lay down close to Tad, and he lifts his am and pulls me closer to him. I breathe in his beautiful smell and try to calm myself down.

The next time I wake it is morning, I can hear birds singing outside, and the smell of coffee is wafting up the stairs. Tad must already be downstairs. I feel awful. I barely slept. Well I fell asleep super quick after sex last night, mainly because I didn't want to face up to what I had said. But I kept waking from bad dreams. I just have this feeling in the pit of my stomach that something bad is about to happen, I'm not usually wrong about this feeling, and I have a hunch it will have something to do with the fact I told Tad I loved him and he said not a word back to me. Nothing! Just that I was beautiful.

So you're upset with him for being normal, and not falling love with you in less than a week?

Oh shut up brain.

I quickly get up, shower and get dressed. I think I could do with a bit of space today. I'll go and spend some of that money Dad sent me and make Ami's room at my parents nice for her.

I walk down the stairs and see Tad deep in conversation with one of his security guards. He sees me coming, pats the guard on the shoulder and walks towards me.

"Morning gorgeous." He says and pecks me on the lips lightly. "How did you sleep?"

"Fine. What was all that about?" I signal to where he and the guard were just talking.

"Well it looks like Kevin is in France."

"France? How would he have got there? Shouldn't the police know that through his passport or something?"

"My men and the police are both looking into it. A card transaction was made from an address in France, but we thought that would be a ridiculous mistake for him to make, as then the police would be able to trace his location. But like I said yesterday, he isn't thinking straight and he is going to make mistakes."

I know Kevin is no Einstein, but he's not stupid either. Something isn't sitting right with me about this.

Tad brings me back from my thoughts by stroking my arm.

"Coffee?"

I smile and nod at him and follow him through to the kitchen.

I take a seat on one of the stools and watch Tad pour me a cup of coffee out. He puts it down and sits down next to me, gently putting his hand on my leg.

"Hey, where's your head?"

"On my shoulders where it's always been." I smile back at him.

"You know what I mean. Are you doing ok?"

"Yeah. I guess. All things considered." I take a sip of coffee and it's perfect, exactly how I like it. I'm so annoyed with myself that I'm more on edge about the whole love business floating around than I am about Kevin. It's actually going to drive me insane if I stay here and I'm going to end up saying something stupid.

"I'm going to go and do some shopping today for Ami's room at my parents, and then I'm going to get everything all set up for her coming back tomorrow."

"Ok. Want me to come with?"

"Uh, I think I'll go by myself babe. Need a bit of me time I think." His face drops. "Don't take it personally, I just need a bit of time by myself."

"Yeah, no of course! I've got some work I need to catch up on anyway. But you'll be back tonight yeah?"

159

I smile at him.

"Of course."

My phone starts ringing from in my pocket, and my heart stops.

Tad hears it, and pulls my phone out for me as I am totally frozen.

"It's just the police station."

Relief floods through me and I answer my phone.

"Hello?"

"Hi, Rachel, its DC Robins. I have some news." My stomach flips, both with excitement and nerves. "We took a look at the CCTV from the store where Kevin's card was used in France. It's quite grainy, but it does look like him. Do you have an e-mail address I can send the image to, so you can see if you agree?"

I hang up after giving him my e-mail, and he tells me that he will send the image straight away.

Seconds later, my phone beeps at me and I see an e-mail from Robins with an attachment.

When the photo eventually loads up I can see why he isn't sure. The image quality is rubbish. I can make out a shop front, a till, a worker and a customer. He is definitely the right build to be Kevin. I can't really see any details on his face. He has a hat on and a coat with the collar up, so it's really difficult to tell. But then I look closer at the coat. It's got random lines running down the arms, and even in the black and white photo I can tell the arms and body are different colours. I remember Kevin coming home with this monstrosity, saying it was totally in trend and that it cost him hundreds. It's him. That's Kevin. In France!

"It's him!" I beam up at Tad. I feel such a weight lifted off my shoulders. There's no way he can hurt me while he is in a different country, and now the police will be on the lookout for him there.

"Are you sure?" Tad squints at the photo again trying to get a better look.

"Yes, I would recognize that awful coat anywhere!"

I quickly call Robins back to let him know it's definitely Kevin.

CHAPTER THIRTY FIVE

Almost £500 later and I walk into my parents' house with enough bags to sink the Titanic.

I've got Ami everything I could think off. New bedding, cushions, soft toys, wall stickers, curtains. An entire new bedroom set.

It feels strange walking into my parents' house knowing that I am going to be moving back in.

I never thought I'd be back living here. Mind you I never thought most of my life would go the way it has. I don't know why this surprises me!

Their house is beautiful and homely. Varnished floorboards cover all of downstairs, with the exception of the shiny black tiles in the kitchen. The furniture is all solid pine, and the sofa is a beautiful cream leather. There is a huge fireplace in the front room. I remember all the Christmases I spent here, Mum would hang all of our stockings over the fire place and we would leave water and carrots for the reindeer and sherry and a mince pie for Santa. I remember questioning it one year, saying that Santa had to drive a sleigh around all night so we shouldn't be giving him alcohol in case he gets pulled over for drink driving.

Yes, I was that kid!

We always gave a glass of milk after that. Even late into my teens Mum would still put it all out, and if I ever dared say I knew Santa wasn't real she would argue until she was blue in the face that he was, and it would always end with her saying if I didn't believe I wouldn't get any presents! I had such a happy childhood here. This place has such a comforting feel to it, and I feel instantly calmer just being back home. I drag all of my bags up the stairs to Ami's room and get started.

Tad

I put my debit card back in my wallet as the lady at the end of the phone confirms my booking details.

"So that is the Superior Suite with dinner at the restaurant, and a full body massage for one booked in for tonight. Dinner is between six and nine pm, and I can arrange your massage for any time before or after. Just let me know when you check in. Is there anything else Mr. Turner?"

"No, thank you very much, you've been very helpful."

"Not a problem. We will see you late on then."

"Bye."

"Goodbye Sir."

I'm such a fucking idiot. I haven't heard from Rachel all day. I know she is upset about the whole *I love you* thing, when I said fucking nothing. Not even one of those awkward as shit *Thank you's* people throw out when they don't reciprocate the feeling. When the truth is I do fucking love her.

There is no point trying to deny it to myself any longer. I love her. And it's ridiculous, and it makes no sense. But isn't that kind of what love is?

I'll tell her tonight.

Fuck this is crazy!

I call her number to see what time to expect her.

"Hey you." She sounds happy.

"Hey gorgeous. How was shopping?"

"Oh it was great! I feel a bit bad I spent so much, but I did get loads for Ami's room."

"What about yours?"

"Well I have a bed in there, I don't really need anything else."

"Well I suppose you will be sneaking out and staying with me most nights anyway?"

"Oh, will I?"

"Yeah, you will miss me too much."

She giggles at me.

"Oh, will I?!"

"Or maybe I will miss you too much."

"Yeah probably!"

"Any idea what time you're going to be back? I have something special planned?"

"Something special?" She sounds intrigued.

"Yes, and it's a surprise."

"Well in that case I can be back in about an hour, two tops. Is that ok?"

"Of course it is. I will see you then beautiful."

I have no idea how I am going to tell her. I'm so nervous this is stupid.

I go up to my room and throw some of my clothes on my bed, then I go into the spare room and try to find some clothes for Rachel. As I look through her underwear I realise she really wasn't kidding when she said about Celine having an ulterior motive when she packed. I *really* must thank her. I pull out a tiny red lacy bra and a matching set of knickers. I quickly find a pair of jeans and a pretty floral shirt for her to wear tomorrow, and I accidentally on purpose *forget* any pyjamas so she has to sleep naked. I smile to myself at the thought.

CHAPTER THIRTY SIX

Rachel

I stand back and admire my work and I'm impressed. I've gone with a unicorn theme as they seem to be a particular favourite of Ami's at the moment. There are unicorns and fairies dancing on the wall above the bed. Her bed is made up in a beautiful pastel pink and blue quilt and pillow set with little unicorns on it, the curtains are a matching print. And I think I may have gone slightly over the top with the huge unicorn teddy bear in the corner of the room. But if Ami doesn't like it I will happily have it for myself! I snap a photo on my phone and send it to Tad and to my Dad.

I figure I have enough time for a quick coffee before I head back to Tads. I wonder what the surprise is? He sounded excited on the phone. Well at least I haven't scared him off. Although that feeling in the pit of my stomach is back. Dread, complete and utter dread. Which is ridiculous seeing as Tad sounded totally fine on the phone, and has a surprise planned for me.

My phone buzzes with a reply from my dad.

What have you done to my house?! LOL Ami says she loves it though. See you tomorrow Princess xx

I laugh at my Dad's reply. The second I moved out, my room was completely redecorated. Gone were the pink walls and posters of various topless boybands, replaced by cream. Cream everything, Dads favourite colour!

I hear the kettle start to boil behind me and I search the cupboards for some of that dried instant coffee... Bleugh... Beggars can't be choosers I guess! I'll have to get my coffee machine out of my house to bring here. I don't care about anything else, but I need the coffee machine! But then again Ami is going to need stuff. And there is stuff I will actually need. Maybe one day next week I can go round with Dad. What even happens with the house now? I have none of my own money, I have no access to our savings, even though it was me that put most of the money in there from inheritance

I got from my Gran. I can't pay the mortgage, council tax or any of the bills. But the house is in Kevin's name, as far as I'm aware I'm not even on the deeds or anything.

I can feel my heart rate race as I start to panic.

Stop.

Deep breaths.

I close my eyes and take a long breath in. I count to five, then breathe slowly out. Dad will know what to do, hell Tad is super clever, he will be able to help. Come to think of it Danny is an estate agent, he will have some idea, or at least will know someone who will be able to help I'm sure. There is no point in panicking about it. It has happened, and it will get sorted. Me and Ami are safe and have somewhere to stay for now and that is all that matters.

I pour the water into my mug and go to the fridge, only to remember that they haven't been home so there isn't any milk.

Oh well, black coffee it is then. I take a sip and then hear a loud bang from upstairs.

What the hell?

I set my mug down on the side and quickly sprint up the stairs to see the window in Mum and Dad's room is wide open. A breeze has knocked the curtain into a cup that was on the windowsill and it's smashed on the floor.

Was that window open earlier?

I definitely didn't see it earlier? But then again the door was closed most of the way and I didn't look in.

I'm just about to start picking up the bigger bits of broken cup when I hear another bang, this time from downstairs.

Fuck, there's someone in the house.

I pick up the biggest piece of sharp ceramic I can find and walk slowly towards the stairs. I pat my pockets down looking for my phone and then remember I left it on the kitchen counter. I start to walk slowly down the stairs, being as quiet as possible. I turn my back towards the wall and lean against it as I walk down the stairs, so that I can check all around me. Nothing looks obviously out of place. I get to the bottom of the stairs and keep my back against the wall of the hallway as I slide into the kitchen. I have my broken shard of mug in my hand and I stretch my arm out in front of me. I'm shaking all over and can hear my heart beating in my ears. I peek my head around the kitchen and see a load of papers on the floor and a fridge magnet next to them.

Jesus Christ Rachel.

The bang was just a magnet falling off the fridge. Obviously when I slammed the fridge door shut I must have knocked it.

I let out a huge sigh of relief and put my ridiculous make shift weapon on the counter next to the fridge. My heart is still pounding in my chest. I feel totally stupid. I'm so on edge right now I probably shouldn't be anywhere alone. I'm just going to head straight back to Tad's before I drive myself totally bonkers.

I quickly bend down to pick up the papers that have fallen on the floor and as I stand back up I hear a loud deep buzzing sound, I am so on edge and jumpy that I actually scream.

At my phone. I screamed at a text alert on my phone.

"Oh my God woman. Get a grip!" I mutter to myself.

I pick up the phone and can't help but smile as Tads name flashes on my screen.

I take it Ami likes unicorns then? Or is that your room? It looks great. See you soon beautiful
xx

I put my phone down and feel my anxiety soften a little. Just a few minutes in the car and I will be back in Tad's arms, where everything seems better.

"Naww. Is loverboy missing you?"

My brain, heart, breathing, everything just stops. I can't move, I'm absolutely frozen to the spot. I would recognize that voice anywhere.

"Aren't you going to say hello Rach?"

Fight or flight. Fight or flight.

I know I can't just stand here. I slowly turn around and there is Kevin.

He looks a state. His eyes are blood shot, his skin dirty, he hasn't shaved and his hair looks greasy and messy.

He is wearing a plain black jacket, not one I've seen before, and definitely not the one from the CCTV image.

He takes a step towards me, and my eyes dart behind him to wear I left the broken shard of mug. If I just duck under him I could grab it and maybe try to cut his face with it. It wouldn't do any damage but might be enough to distract-

He follows my eyes to the counter and sees the piece laying there. He wanders towards it and picks it up.

Tut tut tut.

"I hoped you would just make this easy for the both of us Rachel."

I frantically look around the kitchen for a knife, a fork, anything. Why is there nothing on the side? My steaming hot cup of coffee is just behind me. If I am quick enough I can grab it and throw it in his face, which will give me enough time to run.

He takes an angry step towards me.

Keep him talking!

"Why are you back Kevin? You could have just disappeared."

"I told you. I'm going to kill you. Probably. To be honest I haven't decided yet. It might be more fun to fuck around with that rich cunt. Maybe torture him a bit."

He takes another step and then stops as if he is deep in thought.

"Maybe I could cut off some of your hair and send it to him. And then maybe a finger. He might go all Brad Pitt. *What's in the box?!*" A maniacal laugh erupts from his throat and I realise he has completely lost it. There is absolutely no trace left of the man who I married. I don't recognise this crazy person in front of me, and that is the most terrifying thing.

I quickly feel around behind me for my coffee while he is distracted. I feel the hot cup, grab it and throw the steaming coffee in his face. He yells and covers his eyes so I try to run. But my stupid jelly legs just won't move fast enough. He grabs the top of my arm and pulls me towards him. I grab his arm and dig my nails in as deep as I can while trying desperately to pull away from him.

"Get off me! HELP! Someone"-

He covers my mouth with one of his hands and stifles my screams.

"Shut up for fuck sake Rachel"-

I quickly jolt my head to one side, just enough for one of his fingers to slip in between my lips so I am able to bite down on it. He screams out and I keep biting until I can taste his blood filling my mouth. He manages to get his hand away from my mouth and then wraps his thick arm around my neck. He squeezes so tight I can hardly breathe. I am pounding at his arm and desperately trying to kick behind me but it's no good. I can't get out of this.

From the corner of my eye I see him fumbling around in his pocket.

"You shouldn't have done that you stupid little slut."

Life suddenly slows and I freeze in sheer terror as I see him pull out a needle and syringe from his pocket.

Oh God. This is it.

"Please Kevin! No!"

He grips the cover from the needle in between his teeth and pulls it off.

I give up begging and just scream as loud as I possibly can.

I feel a sharp sting in the side of my neck.

Before I have a chance to think, my head starts to spin, and the blackness starts to creep in. I can't catch my breath.

I am falling into a deep dark abyss and I have no way to stop myself.

I'm surrounded by blackness and the last thing I here is that evil laugh.

I'm so sorry Ami.

CHAPTER THIRTY SEVEN

Tad

I have finished packing all of our clothes and the suitcase is waiting by the door. I try calling her phone for the fifth time. It's been almost two hours since she sent me the photo of Ami's finished room. She should be here by now, and now she isn't answering her phone.

Something is wrong.

I quickly load up her Facebook page and find Celine's profile. I type a quick message to her.

Are you with Rachel? Please call me urgently.

I type in my phone number and click send.

I start pacing my hallway, occasionally opening my door in the desperate hope that Rachel will be standing there waiting for me.

My phone starts ringing and I answer without even looking at who is calling.

"Rachel?"

"No it's Celine. What's going on?"

"Rachel is missing."

"What do you mean missing?"

"She went to her parents to sort Ami's room for her. She sent me a photo about two hours ago of the finished room, so she should have been back here within half an hour. At the very most! Now she's not answering her phone."

I run my fingers through my hair and have the sudden urge to punch something. Why did I let her go by herself?

"You call that detective working on Kevin's case. I will run into town and check anywhere that sells coffee. Don't worry. We will find her." Celine sounds worried too.

"Call me back on this number if you hear anything?"

"Of course, and you."

I hang up the phone and immediately call Robins.

Come on, come on!!

"DC"–

"She's missing." I interrupt. I can hardly even speak I am panicking so much.

"Sorry who is?"

"Rachel! Rachel Blackford! She was at her parents and was supposed to be coming straight back here, but it's been two hours and she isn't even answering her phone."

"Two hours isn't a missing person case."

"It is when your husband is a fucking murderer who has made threats against her!"

"She has probably just been held up somewhere, stay put and I'm sure"–

Fuck this.

Useless prick.

I call Tommo, my head of security.

He answers immediately.

"Boss."

"Tommo, I need someone at my house now. Rachel is missing. I'm going to go out looking for her, but I need someone here in case she comes back. And I need as many people as you can out searching."

"Yes sir. I'll get my men moving now."

I hang up and head for the door. I remember she said her parents lived on a street that's only a couple of minutes down the road. I start sprinting in that direction, checking all the roads and bushes as I go in case she has had an accident.

If that bastard has hurt her I swear I will kill him.

I reach her parents road and pause to catch my breath.

Her car is in the driveway.

Maybe she just fell asleep?

I run as fast as I can to the house.

"RACHEL!!!"

I bang on the door, but as I do it opens.

My heart stops.

"Rachel?"

There is complete silence inside the house and a feeling of sheer terror creeps through me.

I run up the stairs and see all of the rooms are empty. The window in one of the rooms is wide open and the curtain is billowing inside of the room. I turn sharply and race down the stairs. All the rooms are empty again. But then I see it.

A smashed coffee mug, and a fucking needle.

My blood runs cold and I call Robins back again.

"DC"–

"Listen to me, I am at her parents' house. The door was open, her car is outside, yet all that is here is a smashed mug and an empty fucking syringe with a giant fucking needle attached to it. Get here NOW!"

"What's the address?"

I go and sit on the sofa. I feel numb. I can't believe that fucking wanker has managed to do this.

How?

He was in France! This morning! Oh God. He wouldn't really kill her, would he?

I'd better call Celine.

"Have you heard anything?"

"Uh, not as such." The words almost catch in my throat. "I came to her parents' house. Her car is here. The door was open, and there's a smashed mug in the kitchen. And a needle." I almost whisper the last part. The implications of that empty syringe are almost too much for me to bear.

"Holy- What- Fuck. I'm coming."

She hangs up and I sob. I sob like a fucking child.

I had finally found her.

I had spent my entire life looking for her without even realising it. And I finally find her and she is snatched away from me.

Stay positive. He wouldn't kill her.

Wouldn't he?

A few minutes later and there is a frantic banging on the door.

"Tad, let me in!"

For a split second I dared to hope it was Rach, but it's Celine.

I open the door and she pushes past me, straight to the kitchen.

"Don't touch anything." I say quietly. "Robins is on his way."

She turns to look at me and her eyes are red and filled with tears.

Minutes pass. Or maybe hours. I honestly can't tell. Robins told me and Celine to wait at my house for either her or any news. The police and my men are out searching and I just feel utterly helpless.

Celine's an absolute mess. She is sitting on my sofa with a cup of what must by now be stone cold coffee in her hands. I have only known Rachel for a tiny fraction of the time she has, and if it hurts me this much I can't even imagine what she must be going through.

Her boyfriend Dan is sitting next to her, she called him not long after we got back to my house and he raced straight here. He seems like a nice guy. He keeps trying to offer words of support to Celine, but they are met by utter silence.

I'm pacing the floor when I hear banging at the door. Dan shoots up as I race to the door. I open it to find Scott standing there.

"I came as soon as I could man. What's happened?"

I open my mouth to try to speak but nothing comes out.

"It's ok, let's get in and get you a drink."

I close my mouth and go to shut the door.

"Oh hang on." Scott says. "Suze is just getting out of the car."

"You told Suze?!"

"She was with me when you called!"

I sigh loudly and am visibly annoyed. I do not need a thousand questions from her at this moment in time. I look out of the door and see her walking up my driveway.

"Thaddeus! What on earth is going on?!" She holds out her arms to me and pulls me into a tight embrace. Well as tight an embrace as a five foot nothing tiny woman like her can give.

She pushes straight past me and heads for my kitchen.

"Kitchen you two, now."

I shut my door and Scott shoots me a look as if apologising.

I'm not sure if Suze doesn't see Celine and Dan in my front room, or if she doesn't care, but she walks straight on through into my kitchen.

I pull Scott in to introduce them.

"This is Celine, Rachel's best friend, and this is Dan, her boyfriend."

Celine stays completely still, barely even blinking, but Dan holds his hand out to shake Scotts.

"This is Scott, he's my business partner, and that crazy lady is my assistant."

"KITCHEN!" We hear Suze yell at us, and excuse ourselves as we walk through to meet her.

She has three tumblers out and is pouring a small amount of whiskey in each.

"I'm not going to pretend I am not hurt by you hiding a relationship from me Tad, I thought you were my friend as well as my boss. However, now is not the time for that. Tell me everything."

I briefly fill her in on how we met, on the fundraiser. I tell her what Kevin was like and how we ended up together and how Kevin was supposed to be in France this morning. Yet all things point to him being the one who has taken Rachel.

She drains her drink in one.

My phone buzzes inside my pocket and I quickly reach inside to pull it out.

"It's from Rachel!"

My hands start shaking as I open the message, and then I feel all the blood drain from my face. I feel sick, and sweaty and have to sit down before I pass out.

"What is it?" Scott asks with panic in his voice.

I don't think I could speak if I wanted to so I put my phone down on the counter with the photo open.

The photo that shows Rachel, unconscious? *Fuck, please just be unconscious...*With that son of a bitch squeezing her cheeks and kissing her on the lips. The caption reads

Till death do us part loverboy.

I manage to compose myself just enough to grab my phone and find Robins name in my phone book.

CHAPTER THIRTY EIGHT

Rachel

I t's dark. Not just dark but pitch black. It doesn't matter how much I try to open or squint my eyes, I cannot see a thing. I try to move my hands to rub my eyes, but they are stuck behind my back. I can't move them at all. I try to move my feet and they are stuck tight too.

It suddenly dawns on me that my hands and feet are tied up and I am blindfolded. Images flash through my head, unicorns, coffee, Kevin and a needle.

Fuck! Kevin took me.

I start to hyperventilate as I realise the situation I am in. I remember him plunging a needle into my neck, and then that's it. I have no idea where I am or how long I was out.

I try to calm my breathing and listen, for anything. All I hear is total silence. No rustling, or even breathing, so wherever I am I think I am alone. I feel around underneath me, the floor feels rough, almost like really old, dirty carpet. There is a smell of damp and mud lingering in the air. I move my legs out slowly in front of me to try to see how much space I have. I manage to stretch them all the way out, so I don't seem to be in any enclosed space. I can hear my heart beating so loudly and I feel the adrenaline pumping through me. I use all the strength I can muster to try to sit up. It's definitely not easy with no hands or feet to help.

I manage it and I'm able to sit straight up with my legs stretched out in front of me.

I'm absolutely wracking my brain for something, anything to help me right now. Somewhere in the very depths of my mind I remember a video I saw somewhere on the internet about how to free your arms when trapped in this situation. God why did I not pay closer attention.

I'm pretty sure the idea is to try to move my arms under my bum, and then pull them over my legs. At least that way I would hopefully be able to undo my feet to give me a chance of running.

I gently lay myself down onto my back and desperately try to wiggle my huge arse through the gap in my arms.

Why the fuck does my arse have to be so fucking big.

That is not working at all. I sit back up and try to pull my arms as far apart as possible. It feels like they have been taped. If I can just stretch the tape enough I might be able to slip out of it. I clench my eyes and my jaw and I pull with absolutely everything I have. I think of Ami and of Tad. Of my parents. I cannot leave them all behind.

I can feel my arms managing to move further and further apart, only slightly but it might make all the difference. I move them back together and the tape is so much looser now. I try to grip hold of part of the tape with one hand and pull the other out. It's coming! I can feel it! Finally it slips out and it tingles as the blood rushes back to it. I quickly remove my blindfold and after my eyes take a couple of seconds to adjust I realise I am in the back of a van. There are dirty blankets in one corner of it, and a load of food wrappers next to it. The floor is covered in mud and leaves. I move into the middle of the van and look out of the front window. There are clothes on the passenger seat, and more empty food packets. Outside I see nothing but trees. I could be anywhere. I have absolutely no idea. I can't see any sign of Kevin anywhere.

Rachel you don't have time for this. Just untie your feet and get the fuck out of here.

I quickly feel around at the tape on my feet for an end. I finally find it and desperately try to peel the tape apart. Out the corner of my eye I see one of those plastic forks you get in salads. I grab it and snap it in half leaving a sharp point. I stab in at the tape in between my ankles and it goes through. I stab a few more times and then pull my feet apart with everything I have. The tape starts to split, and eventually completely tears apart.

I keep hold of the broken fork.

Cos that's really going to help.

Brain, if you have nothing helpful to say, shut the fuck up.

I need to think. I need to get out of here and run, but run where.

And what if Kevin is outside the van doors.

I search around the back of the van to see if there is anything I could use as a weapon or if he has by chance left a phone laying around.

I pull the carpet up at one the back corner by the door, and find a compartment. I open it up and bingo! Tools! I grab the biggest spanner in there and start to run though the plan in my head.

Quickly slam open the doors to surprise him if he is there. If he is, smack him round the head with this and then run as fast as possible. If I manage to get away from him then I'll keep walking until I get somewhere, or hear cars and then flag someone down.

My heart is racing in my chest and I take a few breaths to try to steady myself.

I grab the handle and start to doubt myself.

He is so much bigger and stronger than me. If he gets me...

Stop thinking like that. You have to give this a try. Think about Ami.

The thought of my beautiful little girl is just enough I need to make me grip the handle and open the door. I throw it open with as much force as I can and jump out, spanner held out in front of me ready to hit him.

Only he isn't there. I take a second to take a look around. There really is nothing but trees anywhere. There must be a road nearby or else he wouldn't have been able to drive here.

I strain my ears for any car noises, but instead I head a twig breaking from behind me.

I spin around so fast it almost makes me dizzy, spanner outstretched and I go to hit him with it.

But he is too fast and too strong. He grabs the arm with the spanner in one hand and uses the other to snatch it away from me.

Tut tut tut.

"Oh Rachel. Now that's not very nice is it?"

He pushes me over on to the floor and crouches down next to me, throwing the spanner behind him.

I am utterly terrified, but I will be damned if he sees that.

"What do you want Kevin?" I ask as matter of factly as I can manage.

"Do you know, I'm not even sure anymore. It used to be you. It was always you Rach. From the second I saw you I knew I had to have you for my own. You were this sweet, innocent looking thing and I knew you were completely untouched and would be totally mine in every way." He edges closer and starts stroking the bottom of my leg. His touch makes me feel physically sick. "Pity you didn't feel the same. I had to force us together in every single way."

This confuses me?

"What do you mean?"

"Well I was ready to settle down, and I knew it would be the best thing for us, but you weren't. You still wanted your single friends and your single lifestyle. Hence why I had to mess around with your pill."

He starts laughing to himself.

"You did *what?*"

"Ah shit, I mean, I'm surprised you didn't work it out! Condoms and the pill and you still get pregnant? How did you not realise that I'd been poking holes in the condoms and flushing a pill down the toilet a couple of times a week?"

175

The smug smile on his face makes bile rise from my stomach into my throat.

I wouldn't change Ami for anything now, of course, but having a baby that young completely changed my life. And left me stuck here. How *dare* he?

I try as hard as I can to not let him see how much this has affected me.

"But... *Why?*" I ask as calmly as I possibly can.

"I knew you'd agree to move in and get married if you had my baby. It was the only way I could get you completely. But you were still so fucking difficult. Never happy no matter what I did for you."

"So you gave up on trying to make it work and instead fucked other women behind my back and made my life a living hell?" I can't help it now. I'm furious and he can tell.

"Well, yeah. I guess you could put it like that. You couldn't give me what I wanted so I got it elsewhere. I still kept a roof over your head, gave you money, what more could you have wanted?"

"How about a life of my own?! Freedom?! I never wanted to be with you, and you didn't even want me from so early on, so why stay?"

"Because you are mine. I made you a woman, and so you will always be mine."

Now it's my turn to laugh. The smile disappears off of his face and he shoots daggers at me.

"What's so fucking funny?" He growls at me.

"Just that you think you made me a woman!"

Rachel, what are you doing?

What was it Tad said, about people making mistakes when they are angry? Well I can make him angry. And hey, if I'm on my way out anywhere then I'm going to fucking enjoy bringing him down a peg or two before hand.

"Of course I made you a woman! You were just an innocent little virgin when I found you. I fucked you, married you and had a kid with you."

"You abused me and lied to me at every turn! You may have taken my virginity, but that is it. If I have anyone to thank for making me a woman it's Tad."

There is it. His eyes flash, and his cheeks turn an intense shade of red. His jaw tightens.

"What, did you say?" He says through gritted teeth.

You've started now. Finish it.

"You heard me. Having sex with you was just, *meh,* something I had to do as your girlfriend. And wife. Sex with Tad is just... *Mmmm.*" I moan lightly and watch as Kevin's entire face turns scarlet and a vein pops out of the side of his head.

"It's raw, and passionate, and he's incredible. Between me and you, I'm pretty sure he could make me come just by telling me to. And, while we are being so honest, I faked *every* one with you."

That worked.

He opens his mouth and lets out a loud roar that echoes around all the open space around us.

There's my cue. While he is distracted I scurry around behind him to find the spanner. I just manage to grab it with my fingers when I feel Kevin's huge hands grab my ankle. I start kicking out as hard as I possibly can. He is pulling me towards him. I grip the spanner tightly and turn around. I swing it as far back as I can and then aim it straight for his face. It connects with this nose with such force that I hear a definite crack. He lets go of me and clutches at his face, screaming.

"My fucking nose!"

I stand up and he tries to grab me again, but I'm too fast for him this time. I swing the spanner down with every ounce of strength I can muster, it smashes down on the top of his head and the thud is so loud it makes me jump. His hand drops, and his eyes lose focus. He drops back down to his knees and then falls backwards, smashing his head once more on a large rock on the floor.

I have absolutely no idea if he is unconscious, and I don't stay to find out. I run as fast as my legs can carry me. My lungs are burning and my legs ae in agony from where I am running so fast but I daren't stop, or even slow. I see a thick bush in front of me and I head into it to hide and catch my breath.

I push my way through the branches and leaves and find as big a space as I can. Bent over, with my hands on my knees I desperately try to catch my breath.

I peek out of the bush and can't see Kevin.

You probably killed him.

Good.

Once my breathing has slowed back to almost normal, I try to stay as quiet as I can to see if I can hear anything at all.

Just birds tweeting and the rustle of leaves in the wind.

I push my way through the other side of the bush and see a clear field of grass. On the very far side of the field is a road.

Thank Fuck!

I jog towards it and start to follow it. The road is absolutely dead, but maybe there will be an emergency phone, or a house or something further up.

I must have been walking for miles. I am freezing and it is starting to get dark. I see lights in the distance and my heart leaps!

The sight spurs me on and I break into a run. The muscles in my legs are on fire and begging me to stop, but I have to get to a phone.

Finally the lights get closer and closer, and I see a little country pub.

Tears start streaming down my face as I realise I did it. I'm alive. I got away!

I burst in through the doors of the pub. It's beautiful inside. In any other circumstances I'd love to sit in here for a drink in front of the roaring fireplace. It's almost empty except for a couple of little old men in the corner. Drinking pints of lager, with their dogs sitting next to them.

A kind looking lady from behind the bar rushes over me to me to ask if I am ok.

"I need to use your phone, please!" I sob at her.

CHAPTER THIRTY NINE

Jess, the lady from behind the bar has sat me next to the fire, wrapped me in blankets and got me a cup of coffee.

Two paramedics have been and looked me over. They are satisfied I am ok, but want me to have more bloods taken tomorrow to check what I was injected with is out of my system. A few random police officers have been in and out, each asking me different questions. Trying to get me to remember where I was, what direction I came from. I can hardly think straight anymore.

Another officer walks over to me.

"Rachel?"

I turn and smile weakly at the officer. He takes a seat opposite me.

"I have been on the phone to the Hampshire force. They passed a message along to DC Robins, and he has just called and asked me to bring you home."

Something twists in my stomach.

"This is going to sound awful, but could I please speak to DC Robins myself to confirm with him?"

"Of course. You've been through quite an ordeal. I'll phone him now for you."

I have no idea who I can trust at the moment. I don't even know where I am.

The officer takes a phone out of his pocket and starts dialing. A minute later he hands the phone to me.

"Hello?"

"Rachel, I am so pleased you are ok."

I sign inwardly, it's him.

"I'm with Mr. Turner and he"- I can hear a rustle on the end of the line, and Tad's voice in the distance.

"Give me that!"

I half laugh to myself.

"Rachel?"

"Tad!" Oh my God it feels so good to hear his voice. I never thought I'd hear it again. I burst into loud, ugly sobs.

"Oh my God Rachel, are you ok?"

"Yes! No! Oh God! I don't know. Tad. I didn't think I'd ever see you again." I can hardly speak through my sobbing.

"I know. I thought... It doesn't matter what we thought, you're ok. Now get in the car with the police and they are going to bring you back to me."

My heart warms at the thought of Tad holding me in his arms again.

"Robins wants to speak to you again, I'll see you soon ok?"

I nod. I know he can't see me, but I'm too overwhelmed to even speak.

"Ok, Rachel." Robins has taken the phone back. "The gentleman standing next to you is Chris. He is an officer with the Derbyshire Constabulary" –

Huh?

"Derbyshire? Where the hell am I?!"

"You're in a place called Hollow Meadows, in the Peak District."

Fuck.

We came to the Peak District for our honeymoon.

"Anyway," Robins continues "Chris is going to bring you back, and I am going to wait here for you. I know it's soon, but I just need to ask you a couple of questions. I have already sent a team up to liaise with the police there, and Chris has sent men out looking for Kevin. We will find him."

I hope they find a body.

The car drive back is insanely long and I fall asleep. Chris gently calls my name and wakes me. I jump and briefly panic as it takes me a moment to process where I am.

"Sorry, it's just me." He sees how shaken I am. Its pitch black outside, but I would recognize that huge glass wall anywhere. My heart practically leaps out of my chest. All the houses along the street are pitch black. I look at the time and see why. 1.55am. There is light coming from Tad's front room though.

Chris walks round and opens the door for me. He helps me out of the car which I am so grateful for as my legs are so sore from all the running. I try to take a step in front of me but my leg almost gives way completely under me. Chris takes my am and wraps it around his shoulders and helps me walk away from the car.

He shuts the door behind him and the loud bang echoes through the street.

Suddenly Tad's front door flies open with such force I worry the door might fly of the hinges.

Tad stands there staring at me, before he runs over and lifts me into his arms.

I throw my arms around his neck and start to weep uncontrollably into his neck.

"Ssshh Rach, baby, it's ok. You're home now."

I look over at Tad's door and I see Celine standing there in Dan's arms. She is sobbing into him. Then behind them is Scott, and the little lady with the red glasses.

Robins finally leaves after what feels like hours and hours of questions and note taking. Scott and Susan give Tad a huge hug and say their goodbyes.

Celine is still cuddled up to me on the sofa and Dan has to practically prise her off of me.

And finally it's just me and Tad.

He comes to sit next to me on the sofa. I turn towards him and crawl onto his lap. I lay my head against his chest and wrap my arm around the back of his neck.

He is running his fingers through my hair and I can feel myself drifting in and out of sleep.

"Rach?"

"Mhmm." I answer sleepily.

"I'm so sorry."

I lift my head to look at him.

"Sorry for what?"

"For being an idiot?"

"When were you an idiot?"

"Rach, you could have died." His voice breaks slightly and I can see his eyes fill with tears. "And to make it so much worse, you would have died without knowing that I love you too."

I just smile at him and stroke his face as he speaks.

"Because I do. And I knew it even before you said it! I was just so scared. I've never felt this way before. And it's all happened so fast. But I am absolutely, head over heels in love with you Rachel. I honestly don't know what I would have done if..." He trails off.

I press my finger to his lips.

"Ssshh. It's ok. I'm back. And I love you."

"I love you too."

I lean in and kiss him gently on the lips.

I can't help but feel hopeful that I might have finally found my happy ending. Except this isn't the end. This is just the beginning...

*Keep your eyes peeled for the next instalment of Tad and Rachel's story in the next book, **Our Life**.*
Please like my Facebook page to be kept up to date.
www.facebook.com/d.gourlay.writer

Printed in Great Britain
by Amazon